THE HOUSE AT
ADAMPUR

Anand Lall

THE HOUSE AT
ADAMPUR

A Story of Modern India

NEW YORK 1956   ALFRED A KNOPF

Drawings by John Teppich

L.C. catalog card number: 56–6649
© Arthur S. Lall, 1956

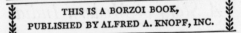

THIS IS A BORZOI BOOK,
PUBLISHED BY ALFRED A. KNOPF, INC.

FIRST EDITION

Part One

CHAPTER ONE

"Be a stone!
Be an axe!
Be insuperable gold!
So live a hundred autumns!"

DEWAN RAM NATH repeated the words softly under his breath, nodding his head with the beat of the syllables while his son, Dina Nath, chanted the invocation.

It was the naming ceremony of Ram Nath's first grandson. The gay, many-coloured, and festooned marquee on the back lawn of the house was filled with the elite of Delhi, including the Chief Justice and, next to him, Pandit Dharma Das— the leading lawyer of the city, who sat in his chair with the air of Lord Roberts of Kandahar on his military charger. He was a large, portly man with a full Georgian moustache and striking grey eyes under heavy brows. His wife, Shanti Devi, stout but dignified, and their daughter, Lena, a strikingly beautiful girl of seventeen, were by his side. Mother and daughter were both dressed in exquisite silk saris of white and gold. Shanti Devi wore a mass of heavy gold inlaid jewelry, while Lena, being unmarried, wore practically none.

Dina Nath, dressed in spotless white and sitting by the sacred fire into which, from time to time, he poured an oblation of butter-fat, continued the invocation for his infant son:

> *"Indra give thee the best of treasures*
> *And bestow them also on us,*
> *O bountiful One, O speedy One!*

On the other side of the sacred fire sat the family priests. They began the recitation of auspicious verses from the Vedas, for the time had come to pronounce the name of the child. A number of servants quickly went among the guests with silver platters heaped with flower petals. Then, as Dina Nath pronounced the name "Chandra Kumar," everyone showered flower petals on the infant and his parents.

The priests chanted louder and kept turning their eyes to Dewan Ram Nath as if to impress upon him the effort they were making on behalf of his grandson. His eye fell on them for a moment, but quickly he turned away with irritation at their mercenary, beseeching look.

Dina Nath chanted the final invocation:

> *"May Saraswati give thee intelligence,*
> *Entwining it with the lotus. . . .*
> *Thou, Chandra Kumar,*
> *Produced from limb by limb,*
> *But of the heart thou art born.*
> *Thou indeed art the self called son!*
> *So live a hundred autumns!"*

Dewan Ram Nath got up and straightened his small, wiry figure. He passed one hand over his pointed grey beard and adjusted the red rose in the lapel of his grey frock coat. His handsome, restless face looked drawn and pale. The excitement of the morning had been too much for his sixty-seven years. He sighed. Then, trying to look composed, he turned to his guests.

All of them had risen from their chairs and many were already hurrying away to their cars. Most of them offered a perfunctory congratulation to Ram Nath, but some, in their eagerness to get away, did not even stop for common courtesies. There was the impatient sound of the quick acceleration of cars on the freshly laid gravel of the driveway, and soon the place was nearly empty.

Ram Nath found himself facing broken rows of empty chairs and a mosaic of strewn, crushed flower petals. He sighed again and looked to see if Geeta, his beautiful niece, was in sight. Ram Nath doted on the girl and thought her the most beautiful and the cleverest young person in the world. She had come from Lucknow especially for this occasion. Her mother, Ram Nath's sister, had died two years before, and she lived with her father, Pandit Brij Krishen, a wealthy lawyer and a member of the inner circle of nationalist leaders. Disappointed at not finding her, Ram Nath decided to go to his study, where he thought he would attempt to straighten out the confusion of the chairs by appealing to the cosmic order as interpreted by Eddington.

The departure of the honoured guests was the signal for the poor of the neighbourhood to come through the narrow gaps in the hedges and over the low back wall, and to crowd around the south veranda of the mansion. Rajeshwari, the Dewan's wife, gave each a bag of sweets and one of nuts. What was left over, after all had been served, was shared among the servants.

For Rajeshwari, the naming ceremony was not connected

with the cosmic plan. It was merely part of the routine of life—and it was important that the routine should be faithfully observed. The kinsfolk and the closest friends had not yet left, and they would expect to be served a specially delicious meal, which, nevertheless, the hostess would suggest was no more than happened to be ready that day for the household. The antiphony would also be enacted. Although none of the guests had any intention of leaving without being fed—and they could hardly wait to see whether the feast was up to expectations—many of them would want to be persuaded to partake of it. To these and other intricacies of the situation, the hostess now turned her attention.

One of the Dewan's cousins who was staying for the feast had brought with him a well-established young lawyer who was also a prominent political figure in the Freedom Movement. He had introduced him to Ram Nath, saying:

"Dewan Sahib, this is Jai Singh of Gurdaspur District."

"Of Gurdaspur? Not, by any chance, the son of my dear friend Prem Singh, of Harbanspura?" asked the Dewan, smiling expectantly.

Jai nodded and smiled assent—which sent the Dewan off again. "Welcome, welcome, Jai Singh. The son of Prem Singh is a son in this house!" And turning to his cousin, he said: "Take your friend and introduce him to all our kinsfolk."

And so Jai, the brilliant young lawyer with his Rajput heritage and background of a North Indian village, was introduced to all the ramifications of this aristocratic, city-dwelling Brahmin family. In the style adopted by Gandhi's associates, Jai was dressed entirely in white hand-spun cotton material—shirt, loose trousers, and a short jacket. He was well built and darker-skinned than the members of this

Brahmin household—wheat-coloured, as the men of the Punjab proudly say. Under his thick black hair was an intense but rather shy, pleasing face; his eyes were very bright, and his well-formed lips seemed always about to break into a smile.

CHAPTER TWO

IT WAS Dewan Ram Nath's unalterable custom to sit down to a meal some fifteen minutes before the rest of the household and any guests who might be present. He was at his fourth meat dish, the one flavoured with dried plums from Bokhara, when the others came in. He looked up, and his quick glance picked out Geeta.

"Come here, child, this is your place," he said, motioning to the chair on his right.

That was the only seating injunction Ram Nath gave. The other guests were waiting for Jag Mohan, the senior kinsman present, to go to the chair on the left of the Dewan, but a dashing young captain, who had been at Sandhurst, was a man of action. He rushed up and took the place so that he could look directly at Geeta.

Several servants came in carrying large gleaming silver plates on which the first serving had been laid for the guests. In the centre of each plate was a helping of saffron-scented pilaff with nuts, raisins, and tender lamb ribs. In a dozen small silver bowls, laid along the inner rim of each large plate, were curried lamb gristle, grilled partridge with a faintly sour sauce, lamb flavoured with orange and sugar crystals, meat balls with a centre of Bokhara plums, bar-becued lamb ribs, curried chicken, pheasant, lamb cooked with turnips, curried okra, spiced lotus stalk diced, two or three lentils, and two preparations of yogurt. On the plate were also two puris, some condiments, and sweets. Over the heaping rice in the centre of the plate gleamed a fine fila-ment of pure silver—finer than a ten-thousandth of an inch thick and, of course, edible. Jai was amazed at the lavishness of the feast. On even the most festive occasion in his village he had never seen anything like it.

For the first few minutes, he noticed, there was not even an attempt at conversation. Everyone ate with relish, but Jai found himself distracted by Lena, who sat almost directly opposite him. He had seen her several times at meetings of the younger political workers, but—like many of the others at the meetings, probably including himself—she had always looked remote. Now in surroundings that were familiar to her, she had come alive, and although he tried to concentrate on his food, he found his eyes returning to her again and again.

Sensing that Ram Nath was not entirely happy at the way the events of the morning had gone, Geeta decided to talk about things completely unconnected with the day's ceremonies or with family affairs. She addressed herself to Shanti Devi, and hearing her voice, Jai half-guiltily turned his face from Lena to her mother.

"Shantiji, is the local Congress Party joining in the demonstrations for Bhagat Singh's release?"

Shanti Devi was upset by this question. Bhagat Singh was a hero among all the young nationalists and also among those of the older generation who wanted a more spectacular policy than Gandhi's constant insistence on truth and nonviolence. Not knowing what might be the decision of the Congress, she thought it wise to take popular feeling into account. She squirmed a little and pouted as she said: "We are calling a meeting next week about the situation; it needs the most careful consideration."

The Dewan looked up, amazement and annoyance in his eyes. He cleared his throat with a little grunt, and in his characteristic quick way he said: "Shanti Devi, you know I have the greatest respect for the Congress, but I must say the local leaders are insane if they are considering what to do about these foolish Bhagat Singh demonstrations. Bhagat Singh was a desperate fellow who took advantage of the situation and won cheap renown by shooting some poor wretched English youth of about twenty who left his country to earn an honest living."

Geeta gasped with amazement. Turning quickly to Ram Nath, she interrupted: "But wait, Uncle, how can you say that an Englishman who comes out here and lords it over our people earns an honest living?"

Ram Nath smiled at Geeta and lowered his voice. "All right, Geeta darling. He should not have been here! But the main point is that the accepted rule of the fight for our independence is non-violence on both sides. I admit that the Government does at times use some violence, but it generally does so with moderation. Bhagat Singh and his friends have violated the accepted rules. And then Shanti Devi—whose leaders have propounded the non-violence rule—tells us that the Congress is going to decide what it should do about the demonstrations for the man on our side who has broken the rule! It just doesn't make sense to me. Indeed, Shanti Devi, if you don't mind my saying so, it's pure nonsense."

"Dewan Sahib, it's all very well to say that, but the people regard Bhagat Singh as a patriot, and that cannot be ignored," said Shanti Devi, rather weakly.

The Dewan was more angry than ever. Stupid and obstinate woman, he thought—it was no use talking to her. So he sighed and addressed himself to the others. "What do you young people think about this matter?" Then he took another quick bite of barbecued spare rib and, munching very fast, he added: "I suppose what you think is going to be much more important than what old men like me do."

Jai was conscious that all eyes had turned toward him as the only representative present of the younger group of political leaders. He glanced at Geeta and saw in her face an insolent, almost derisive challenge. She seemed to expect him to say something—indeed, she almost commanded him to do so, while indicating clearly that really he had no right to speak. Self-consciously, Jai lowered his eyes and brushed aside the look Geeta had given him.

Jai spoke calmly and with an easy flow of words. "Dewan Sahib, the point, really, is—which is deeper among the people, the feeling for freedom or the conviction that we must remain non-violent? I wish I could say that it is the conviction about non-violence, but in fact it is not. So, whatever the Congress may decide, the same people who take part in their programs will tomorrow go out and demonstrate for Bhagat Singh. That is what puts the leaders into a quandary. The best they can do is reaffirm their belief in non-violence and not attempt to tell the people what to do about Bhagat Singh. Even the best rule cannot be forced on people, and certainly not the rule of non-violence."

"Well, that at least is realistic," said Ram Nath, some of his annoyance subsiding.

Geeta had been watching Jai as he spoke, fascinated by the live movement of his lips: what he said seemed so intelligent, and he was undoubtedly very handsome. A swift, grasping enthusiasm for him rose in her, and after Ram Nath's comment she broke out in rather a high tone: "Uncle, that was not just realistic! It was truthful and even idealistic. What Jai means is that you cannot impose an ideal on people. You must go on trying to teach them and go on living the ideal. Isn't that the way?" And now she looked at Jai, bestowing on him her admiration without losing any of her superciliousness.

Ram Nath never argued with Geeta. Besides, he did not want to prolong the discussion, which, as usual, seemed to him to be getting nowhere. So he said: "Yes, my dear, you are right, I think."

Then he prepared to leave the table, for he had finished his lunch and it was not his custom to wait for the others. He wiped his fingers vigorously on his napkin and pushed his chair back.

He went to his rooms wondering to himself. Had he really got nothing quite right? He had his principles, and he thought it the highest virtue to apply them to life. But it did not seem as simple as that. These days it looked as if in each

situation one had to try to apply a number of mutually ill-
fitting principles and somehow get them all in. Well, well,
perhaps it was best for him that he was growing old and
would not be called upon to make important decisions affecting other people. But that comforted him only for a moment.
He was suddenly frightened for himself. What would become of him if he died now in this state of confusion; and
even if he did not die, what would happen to him living
among these new forces and unknown rules of action? He
decided not to read any more of Eddington just yet and to
take a siesta instead.

The luncheon became a much more informal affair after
the Dewan had left. Pandit Dharma Das helped himself
again to most of the score of dishes and, overcome by their
succulent savours, he felt the trials of life imposed on him by
the eccentricities of his wife becoming remote and inconse-
quential. The young captain from the Rajputana Rifles now
smiled almost continuously at Geeta, and that seemed to
please him immensely. Geeta once glanced in his direction
and thought that she had seldom seen anyone look so stupid.
The Dewan's wife went about telling her guests that they
were eating nothing, and some of them responded by filling
their plates again.

Lena had become conscious of Jai's glances and she felt a
flush rising to her face. She, too, remembered having seen
Jai at political meetings in which he played a very prominent
part, and it flattered her that this rising young leader, whom
everyone admired, should now be paying attention to her.
When the meal ended, she hoped he might come up to her,
but her father, Dharma Das, was in a great hurry to return
to his office to interview a prominent and wealthy client, and

Lena and Shanti Devi had to leave with him without even waiting to thank Ram Nath.

For Jai, the room was empty when Lena had left. The talk of the people who filled it did nothing to relieve the sense of bare walls and of the high white ceiling staring down at him. He was glad when his companion rose to leave. Jai went toward Geeta to make his farewell salutations. She came up close as if asserting some right over him. Jai felt the words of thanks freeze on his lips. He could communicate nothing to the arrogant girl who stood before him apparently demanding his submission. When Geeta said: "I am sure my uncle, the Dewan, will invite you again to Dewan House," she expressed a patronizing approval of him which froze Jai all the more. He could say nothing, but tried to smile and nod as he stepped aside to give place to the other departing guests who wished to talk to her. As Jai left, he looked back at Geeta, who stood on the highest pavement of the marble stairs of the front veranda bidding good-bye to her guests. A curious girl, he thought. She was like a strange plant that drew its sustenance from the cold cascade of stone on which she stood. And yet a fire burned fiercely in her which had shed on him some of its sparks.

CHAPTER THREE

THAT NIGHT the lights gleamed from all over Dewan House, picking out every cornice, archway, balcony, and the outer lines of the mansion, which looked immense, seeming to fill half the night with the blaze of its illumination. Thousands of passers-by stopped to wonder at the profusion and gaiety of the spectacle. Many of them were deeply moved and repeated to one another: "The great Dewan is bringing his riches and honours to lay them at the feet of a child a few days old. This is real humility. God will bless him richly. What a night this is!"

No blessing came to Ram Nath that night. He was unable to compose himself for sleep. The brilliance of the day seemed to invade the dark, restful places of the night. He tried to defeat the trouble-making events of the day by going over each step and telling himself that his impulse had not been faulty; he had simply miscalculated the reaction of his guests. None of them had paid any attention to what he

himself considered the central fact: that this was a celebration of creation itself, and that they were giving its manifestation a name. Ram Nath tossed in his bed. Were people no
longer aware of these things? he asked himself. But even
this attempt, justified though it seemed to him, to shift the
responsibility for his sense of failure brought no relief; and
it was only in the anæsthetic hours of the early morning that
he fell asleep with a cold, collapsing feeling in his stomach.

The next morning the Dewan awoke late, and he seemed
to have thrown off the despair of the previous day. He felt a
clear, unimpeded vitality in each movement. He smiled to
himself—a perfect musing ripple of life, and the reflection of
a pleasing idea. He would get his private chauffeur, Raghu,
to drive him out to meet some of his friends. Perhaps he
would even visit that old devil Raja Muzaffar Khan.

Ram Nath decided that it was Muzaffar Khan whom he
would visit, and they drove to his mansion in the old city.
He found the Raja sitting in his library listening to a report
from his Meerut estate. Muzaffar Khan was a well-preserved
sixty-five. His grey hair was brushed back and scented with
rose-water—in fact, rose-water had obviously been sprayed in
the library a little earlier that day. His features were fine and
looked almost Semitic. His medium-sized figure was well
groomed, but his eyes were blood-shot, perhaps from too
much good living. His taste was a little on the loud side—he
wore a large uncut emerald ring and he was smoking from a
gold and inlaid ivory cigarette-holder. As always, he was
immaculately dressed; on this occasion in a suit of soft hand-
woven natural silk—a long buttoned-up coat and tight trousers. He rose to greet Ram Nath.

"Come in, come in, Dewan Sahib. How are you today?
Please sit down while—with your permission—I finish with

Munshiji, who has come from Meerut." And, taking a spiced leaf of pan from a silver case, he gave it to the Dewan.

The Raja fancied himself as a lover of books and a patron of the arts, and here Ram Nath was in the centre of the accumulated evidence. The library contained rows of heavy leather-bound editions of Scott, Dickens, and Balzac; a 1911 edition of the *Encyclopædia Britannica;* well-bound editions of the Indian epics, the Arabian Nights, the Persian poets, and some volumes of Tagore. On the walls hung a dim reproduction of "Hope," a stiffly painted picture of an ascetic sitting in the lotus pose prescribed for meditation, and two shiny prints of scantily clad ivory-and-pink girls. Ram Nath felt somewhat uneasy.

Muzaffar Khan dismissed his manager and turned to Ram Nath with a smile. "You and I, Dewan, are gentlemen of cultivated tastes, and we appreciate the need of man to pay tribute to the finer things of life." He waved his hand lightly toward the walls and went on: "How would it be, then, if we were to go to my little place at Adampur and listen for a while to the singing of the incomparable Ranu? H-m-m? —tell me."

Ram Nath winced. It was his craving for just this sort of venture that had brought him to see the Raja, but how admit that he and that old devil Muzaffar had anything in common? He half sighed and half smiled, and dragged out words that he could hardly believe when he heard them:

"Well, since you were preparing to go, it would be boorish of me to disrupt your plan. Let us go, Raja Sahib."

Muzaffar Khan laughed heartily at his friend's effort to deceive himself. "All right, Ram Nath, all right, put it that way if you must; and if you enjoy the evening, don't let yourself admit it!"

❀

They drove to the Adampur estate in Muzaffar Khan's limousine, of which all the windows were tinted a deep blue so as to give the occupants complete privacy. After driving about twenty miles on the macadamized trunk road, they turned on to a beaten earth track alongside an irrigation canal. Ram Nath knew that this road was reserved for the use of the senior inspecting officers of the Irrigation Department of the Government, and he looked around uneasily while his mind spelled out the situation: "You see where you are. This old fool, the Raja, has no right to use this road, and what if now you are both caught and disgraced?" But Muzaffar Khan, proud of his right-of-way on this closed track, set at rest Ram Nath's immediate fears by explaining: "You see, Dewan, I am among the selected few. It is so easy. Each year I send the Chief Engineer a large basket of the choicest mangoes from my estate, and each of his underlings, down to the sub-overseer, gets his due size of basket. So I use the road openly, and no one objects." He shrugged his shoulders. "What is one to do? I don't like doing it that way, but I have to get to my estate."

Ram Nath felt better when they entered the orchard, heavy with the scent of the mango and loquat blossoms, even though the car jolted uncomfortably toward the house on a rough dirt track. Near the house, the track became a brick pavement from which a short flight of steps gained a terrace on which the house itself stood. It was a two-storied building, and in the front wall the only opening was a large wooden doorway with rusty iron studs on its panels, framed in beautifully carved supporting doorposts and a lintel of pink sandstone. As the car approached, the door opened on its creaking, heavy wooden hinges and two servants ran toward the Raja, making as if to help him enter the house.

They completely ignored the Dewan. The Raja waved them aside and, with his friend, entered the doorway.

They went through a passage into a courtyard, then through a veranda to the main building, which also was double-storied. Ram Nath noticed that the outer building, which held the great doorway, looked rather dilapidated—undoubtedly it housed the servants' quarters; it was in the main building, which they had now entered, in complete seclusion from the outer world, that the Raja's own rooms were situated. They walked through the house to a terraced garden with a row of miniature fountains down the centre, from which the softly tinkling water fell into a shallow, lilied trough. The two friends decided that the garden, in the balmy, scented evening, was the ideal setting for the promised entertainment. Muzaffar Khan gave his orders to the servants and the two friends strolled into the garden.

The servants brought a Persian carpet and spread it on the terrace, and at one end they laid a mattress arranged with pillows and bolsters. On the opposite side was laid a smaller mattress with fewer bolsters and pillows. First came the musicians—a drummer and two men with string instruments—who sat down on the carpet near the smaller of the two mattresses. Muzaffar Khan and Ram Nath returned to the terrace and sat against the bolsters and pillows on the large mattress. Two servants followed and withdrew quickly after laying a low table with fruit, nuts, pan, a bottle of Scotch, and some glasses.

Then Ranu emerged from a side door. Ram Nath saw her come rapidly toward them with small tripping steps. At once, in spite of his outer stiff reserve, something in him acknowledged her exquisite gracefulness. She was dark for a North Indian woman. Her face was very finely made and, though she was just barely smiling, a wonderful light seemed to flash from her eyes. She wore a full skirt of soft purple silk satin, a tight bodice of deep-red Bangalore silk, and a fine gossamer-like veil of Banaras silk. She went toward the Raja and, after greeting him, she asked about his health and that of his sons. Her face was still politely listless and the words she chose were of the most formal. She appeared aloof from the whole scene and totally unaware of the presence of the Dewan. Fool that he was to have allowed himself to be drawn into this situation, thought poor Ram Nath. He would gladly have withdrawn and fled home to his struggle with astrophysics. But he felt utterly helpless and surreptitiously clutched at a bolster.

Muzaffar Khan acknowledged Ranu's greetings and expressions of solicitude with the same formality with which they had been addressed to him. This done, his expression immediately changed. He turned to Ranu with a gleam in his eye and, with a peculiar gurgle in his throat, he said: "Ranu, my beautiful one, are you going to tantalize me tonight? No, you wouldn't do that! Sing something, then, that will soothe this old heart of mine and set on fire the young blood of the Dewan. Oh! I forgot to tell you about him. He is famous and very rich—and handsome, don't you think? —but, poor man, he has never known any happiness. Now, at last, he has come here because Ranu can give him all the happiness that his sad body and his soul require—for these things are of the soul, after all." And, saying this, he turned toward the Dewan with his eyes sparkling, and exploded with laughter that shook his whole body.

Ram Nath felt as if he were falling into an endless pit while the Raja and this not very beautiful woman, who must certainly be of very low caste, were enjoying his discomfiture.

Ranu merely smiled at the Raja's words, but an intensely live quality was coming into her face as though she were emerging from another world. It was at this transitional point that Ram Nath felt most uncomfortable. He clung desperately to the placidity which Ranu was abandoning, for to him, in an alien situation, it appeared to be the last vestige of his own world, while the live, glowing thing which she now was becoming seemed to be related to the coarse and rather sinister world of his friend.

Ranu motioned with her hand, and the music began. The quick beat of the drums filled the air with a kind of rhythmic laceration which Ram Nath found strangely soothing. Her face glowing, and one hand raised toward her left ear, Ranu began to sing the melody of the song in a resonant contralto voice. Her notes mingled with a sensuous ease. Ram Nath felt them touching him everywhere. Then she paused briefly, holding the magic in suspense. Just before the mood changed, she raised her head toward Muzaffar Khan and joined the accompanist again, this time singing the words of the song:

"Friend, were you lost last night in sleep—
Were you lost last night in sleep? . . ."

Muzaffar Khan listened, his face presenting an expectant smile. He filled his glass and swallowed some more Scotch. What was this about last night? He could not think where he had been. His memory spun itself out as the last notes of the line died, but he recaptured nothing of the previous night's happenings. Ram Nath listened attentively, but instinctively he recoiled from the question contained in the song. Of course she was just singing a song, he knew, but

this loose woman, he thought, God knows what she is leading up to! After the drums had further cleared the cobwebs
in the air and gently tapped Ram Nath with their sensual
touch, the song went on:

> *"But not the nightingale till morn—*
> *Not the nightingale till morn . . ."*

Muzaffar Khan was pleased. The scene had shifted to the
warbler of the poetic arborage. His life was not being inves-
tigated. He regained interest in the song, his body swayed,
and he nodded approval at Ranu, whose face had reached a
height of intensity and seemed to pulsate in communication
with the music. Ram Nath felt trapped in a bird cage. He
was the dumb nightingale of the moment: not even that, for
he had no wings.

Ranu went on:

> *"Who night-long filled the silent deep—*
> *Night-long filled the silent deep . . ."*

Muzaffar Khan refilled his glass: night-long to fill one's
glass with Scotch; no, night-long to fill the deep with love.
Yes, night-long was the right idea. Ram Nath thought of the
deep interstellar silences. What filled them? He couldn't remember—just imagine not knowing! He strained his memory, but nothing came to mind. Did anything at all fill those
spaces or were they empty? Empty? He was filled with
panic. Could there be emptiness even there? And suppose
that silly woman were to stop singing and ask him, very politely ask: "Uncle, tell me what there is between the stars. I
have always wanted to know. There is something there that
fills me with great happiness—what is it, Uncle?" That is

how she would ask her question, and he would have no answer, and she would look at him with pity. Never in his life had he felt so inadequate. Ranu went on:

>*"To laud the rose of spring, new-born—*
>*The rose of spring, new-born!"*

Beautiful young rose, newly born, and discovered in all her loveliness; and welcomed with song. The preliminaries were over for now, the rose was ready for him. Muzaffar Khan took another gulp of Scotch. He, too, was ready. The rose was waiting for him. Fool, he must not keep her waiting. There she was, singing to him, calling him—beautiful rose, beautiful Ranu, singing to him. She repeated the quatrain:

>*"Friend, were you lost last night in sleep?—*
>*But not the nightingale till morn*
>*Who night-long filled the silent deep*
>*To laud the rose of spring new-born!"*

Muzaffar poured himself some more whisky and, as the drum beat time, he intoned:

>*"The rose of spring new-born—*
>*The rose of spring new-born."*

Ram Nath looked at his friend as if about to ask which rose. This was not the season of roses, any fool knew that. Thank God, here was something he could tell them if they would but ask him. But he heard no question, only Muzaffar Khan saying: "Ranu, my rose, my nightingale, come to me now, let us fill the night." The Raja stretched out his arm toward her. She rose to come. Silently her musicians disappeared into a side door. Two servants appeared and in a moment they spread another mattress a few paces away. On it they put several large soft bolsters, and they opened a folding screen between it and the scene of the singing. Muzaffar Khan was helped to his feet and, with Ranu, he went to the newly laid and now hidden mattress.

Ram Nath was alone. Now he could contemplate the stars if he wished, and rid himself completely of all the madness that he had just been witnessing. For a moment he felt dignity returning to him and a sense of being in possession of the situation. But what situation? There was no situation. All through, they had completely ignored him, and now they had apparently forgotten that he even existed. He shifted his position on the mattress, expecting that a servant might emerge and inquire whether he wanted anything. But there was no movement from any direction, apart from the sounds of movement from the other side of the screen which he was trying to exclude completely from his cognizance. He poured himself a little Scotch—he drank rarely—and sipped it. He ate some nuts and realized that he was hungry. He drank some more and ate all the nuts in the dish. Perhaps they would notice that he had finished the nuts and would replenish the supply. But no, there was no sign of anything at all.

Something kept him from getting up and walking about. He felt certain that if he tried, two men would appear and take him away to an obscure room in the house so that the Raja should not be disturbed. He looked up at the stars. Yes, there were the interstellar spaces, but they were as unanswering and unconcerned as the scene in which he sat. Perhaps, after all, they were really empty; indeed, that was the latest theory, was it not? No, he could not remember. He drank a little more whisky. He felt a pleasant drowsiness fill him. The stars were in their stations and he was in this garden.

The stars and he were silent and unconnected. Space was empty. Of course it was—empty, but very friendly and small. One star had just bent down and touched him. So he got up and bowed and the star smiled. He put out his hand and touched it. . . . Someone was shaking his shoulder. It was Muzaffar Khan saying that it would soon be daylight and they had better be going. Ram Nath struggled out of his sleep. Was it almost morning? All he could remember was a star bursting open and smiling, and as he had stretched out his hand to touch it, he had recognized the smiling face as that of Geeta. What would she think of all this? He must get out of here quickly. He hurried toward the car with Muzaffar Khan.

In the car, the Raja stretched himself and, sitting up, he looked encouragingly at his friend and said: "Ram Nath, this is life. See, this is what you have been missing. You must do this more often. There is no difficulty at all. Just let me know when you want to go out again."

Like a lamb, Ram Nath replied: "Yes, Muzaffar Khan, thank you. I suppose this is life. Yes, of course I will come again." He got home from his visit to life just as the birds were beginning to fill the morning with their calls. Fortunately, no one saw him slip quietly into his room.

CHAPTER FOUR

"YOUNG LEADER! Young leader!" Jai Singh turned around, his eyes trying to conceal the instinctive annoyance he always felt at the form of address now commonly used for him by the Congress Party national workers in Delhi and elsewhere in North India.

It was a youth with a note from Jai's friend Shabir Khan, telling him to come at once to a meeting at which the supporters of Bhagat Singh were pressing for some show of force against the British. Jai's whole body tingled. It was about seven o'clock in the morning and he was fresh from an hour's kabadi and parkaudi by the river—he went out for these games two or three mornings a week with some of the young men in the political movement.

Jai walked rapidly to his two-room apartment shaded by the great peepul trees just inside the Kashmiri Gate of the old city wall. He quickly bathed and changed. Shabir met him at the door of the meeting-room—a small hall attached to the

Raj Narain school. The contrast between the two men made an interesting composition. Shabir was tall and rather lean. He wore an open silk shirt and loose, wide trousers. A lock or two of his long black hair fell on his brow. His large black almond eyes shone with a liquid brilliance heightened by perfectly curved long eyebrows. His hands were finely shaped and long-fingered, and on his feet he wore elegant, soft, brown leather pumps. Shabir Khan was an urban aristocrat, finely bred and sensitive. Jai, too, was sensitive and, in his way, finely bred, but he was bred out of the soil and his whole appearance proclaimed it. He was shorter than Shabir and broader built. A fringe of hair showed under a white Gandhi cap, and his shirt and tight trousers were of white hand-woven material. Jai's handsome features showed strength rather than a fine delicacy. His eyes were small and emitted a concentrated light, almost shaftlike. On his feet he wore simple, rather squeaky strapped brown sandals. He disliked the squeak of the leather, and one of the things he promised himself in the free India was that leather would be cured till it was quiet.

The look in Shabir's face and the few words he said showed that there was no time to lose.

The two men strode rapidly into the meeting-room. Jai heard a heavy-lipped squat young man saying with a kind of sneering proprietary arrogance: "What of that? There is no difficulty at all, the money can easily be provided."

There were enthusiastic nods from some in the room, while others smiled sheepishly and a few looked terribly upset. Lena called out, her fine features quietly tremulous as a bee's wings: "What! Take the money and sell out the Movement, sell out Gandhiji?"

The opposite camp roared with contemptuous laughter,

and as they turned to one another they noticed Jai and Shabir standing near the door. Their laughter stopped short. Uneasily they shifted in their lounging positions and some pretended they had merely been clearing their throats. For a
moment Jai said nothing, letting the silence lie heavily on
their crouching forms. Then he walked into the room and,
turning to Munshi Ram, in a low deliberate voice he said:
"Do tell me, too, about this use of our funds that is being
discussed."

"Not our national funds, young leader. Oh, no! I was going to put up the money myself," said Munshi Ram, smiling obsequiously and hoping that would end the interest Jai
Singh appeared to be taking.

He had miscalculated. Jai was more interested now than
before.

"Must be something important, then, if you are putting up
the money. Tell me what it is." He had spoken a little louder
and with emphasis.

Munshi Ram's face lost what little shape it had. He took
one foot firmly in his left hand as if to hold himself together
and, waving his other arm, he stammered: "Nothing, nothing—no proposal. I was merely going to provide twenty buses
to transport some men to the British residential section of the
town."

"What men?" asked Jai.

Munshi Ram winced under the frank, clear face that Jai
turned on him. He did not know what to say.

Lena broke in. "What men? None of ours! They want to
collect several score of professional toughs and let them loose
in Raisina—I suppose they will assault some poor woman,
burn a car or two, and thoroughly disgrace the Movement
and the name of Gandhiji!"

As Jai listened, a cold shower seemed to drench his solar plexus. He turned again toward Munshi Ram, his face flushed and the veins on his hands pounding against his skin, but still in complete control of himself.

Munshi Ram slithered his heavy posterior along the durrie-covered brick floor and lifted his joined hands in supplication: "It was only an idea, a fool idea," he said pleadingly. "I don't even know which donkey thought it up. Young leader, nothing could have come of it, absolutely nothing."

Jai waited. No one said anything more. He wished they would speak their minds. He wished they would explain all this to him. But there was only silence, a silence that tortured him. He knew it was not just himself personally but also the fact that they believed him to be in the good graces of the great leaders—Gandhi, Nehru, and some of the others—that had shut them up. And before, because he was not there, they had been thinking up some despicable, shameful scheme —probably originated by Munshi Ram. So that, if there were no Gandhi or Nehru, they would probably bow down to Munshi Ram and accept his ways. He shuddered at the conclusion. He looked round at them again, feeling hollow and symbolized. They sat with bent heads—all except those who had opposed the scheme—and Munshi Ram still grovelled at his feet.

Slowly Jai regained a sense of being himself, and something welled up in his hollow insides. He breathed deeply, as if testing himself, and then said in a quiet voice: "Would any of you care to go to the Bhagat Singh demonstration to-morrow?"

Some of those whose heads were bowed looked up, but their frightened eyes seemed to muzzle their faces. None of them spoke. Then Munshi Ram shifted even closer to where Jai stood, and again raised his hands.

"Young leader . . . leader," he stammered, as if asking for permission to continue. "Leader, none of us will go near the demonstration. We were foolish. We didn't know what we were doing."

Lena's look softened. She felt her dark eyes lift her up and draw her toward Jai. As she rose, others too started moving about, some toward Jai and some toward the door. There were a hundred crisscross paths and knots. Lena's eyes lost Jai. With Shabir and two or three others, he left the room. When she reached the door, he was not even in sight.

CHAPTER FIVE

JAI LIKED to do his morning yogic exercises on the soft blue Persian carpet in his living-room. He was standing on his head. The big leaves of the peepul tree outside his bay window seemed to bend right over him. They looked so wide open from underneath and the fine veins ran from the central stem to the edges like a woman's hair opened out. The leaves shook placidly and he felt a little trickle of breeze brush against the moisture that was forming on his chest from the exertion. Now the leaves were like gentle hands stretching out to touch him. He felt the top of his bare feet tingle, and then a delicious drip-drop of sensation trickled to his thighs. He checked the flow and, with an effort, his mind swept aside the images. He tried to concentrate on thinking of the summit of the sweet-smelling hill near the family summer home—the hill against the clean, sun-pouring blue sky; yes, that was restful and relaxed—just as he should be while he kept the shirshasana posture.

But the breeze was still playing slowly with the leaves and once more they were like a woman's delicate hands. Jai slowly bent his knees and brought his feet down to the floor. It was no use going on. He was just not able to concentrate, and what was the good of the standing on his head when his thoughts were persistently centering on other things?

He sat on the carpet in the lotus pose as prescribed for meditation—cross-legged, with his feet drawn over his thighs. He would clear his brain and think things out. He breathed evenly and sat very still. He was just beginning to feel bland and relaxed, a sensation he recognized well. It was the beginning of the calm limpidity that he wanted.

The door pushed open. Shabir was smiling at him and shaking his head. He said: "Jai! Either working or sitting like an ascetic! What sort of a man are you? I bet you never have thought of anything else—of a woman—have you?"

Startled at this impression of himself, Jai sat stock still, feeling that he held down some secret that would burst open like a jack-in-the box if he moved.

"Anyway," went on Shabir, waving his hand, "I am going

to see that there is a change. There's a picnic on tonight.
We've borrowed Raja Muzaffar Khan's garden of love—you
know his place at Adampur—and we are going to have fun.
You'll be picked up at seven. I must rush and get the party
together." Shabir left, his light feet tripping down the stairs.

Then even the lotus pose was no use. Jai resented having
to break his own planned calm, and he did not want to go
to the picnic. But he knew there was no way out. Shabir
would just come himself and fetch him.

Jai felt very sacrificing and remote when two young captains from the Rajputana Rifles and two young women from
Bombay called to drive him out. Jai thought the two men
looked like a pair of young horses bred in the same stable—
their black hair was cut short and parted in the centre, and
they wore closely trimmed narrow moustaches, grey slacks,
white silk sports shirts, and maroon silk scarves with a sub-
dued paisley design. One of the women was round-faced and
round-eyed, and Jai thought she was no more than eighteen
till he noticed that her lower lip had developed a twisted
droop on one side which made her look considerably older.
She kept moving her smooth, long-fingered hands as if she
wanted them to be noticed.

Jai could not see the other woman's face—she sat in the
front seat with one of the young horses. But her laughter was
like a child's, and her voice, too, reminded him of something
out of his own childhood. At first the others entirely ignored
Jai, and everything any of them said made the others roar
with laughter. Jai felt himself trying to smile, trying to show
that he was not remote, while inside he continued to be occupied with his own thoughts. Then the women started
drawing him into the conversation and soon he, too, was
joining in the general merriment.

On the Raja's terrace, several couples were dancing to western music played by a phonograph. The captains and the two young women from Bombay joined in. Jai sat with the hostess, a polite, stout, heavily made-up person whose face shone unpleasantly in the moonlight.

"Don't you dance?" she asked, smiling at him.

He shook his head. But the music and the couples dancing, among whom were Lena and a young man he did not know, were swirling through him. He wanted to get up and whirl around with Lena. He wanted to move swiftly together with her and then swing around and feel the music turning, turning them. But he sat there silently.

The eating and chatter began. Lena sat two removed from him and he kept looking at her. He thought she was aware of him. She got up and passed him something.

They were all to play a game, forming a circle and holding hands. Lena and Jai stood together. He waited till the rest of the circle had been formed, then he took her hand. Immediately there was a live current jumping up his arm. He had not realized it would be like this. The current rose more strongly. He never knew what happened in the game. He was completely taken by surprise. It was all so secret, but so powerful and trusting. She was going right out to him. At once, simply, she was giving herself.

It was like an avalanche coming at him. He remembered no more about the picnic. The laughter and the chatter were now on the other side of a great wall. The wall was really his own. He did not know how to live the new rhythm of love. Deeply moved and elated, he felt himself fumbling. Lena was baffled by him. She drifted away when the game was over and talked to the hostess.

On the way home, Lena and Jai sat together in the car.

Again he felt a warm urgency tingling in him when she touched him, and he was exhilarated and confused. He wanted to take her hand and to put his arm around her, but he did not. Lena wondered at him. He had followed her and now he did not seem to respond to her. She was hurt, but still felt she wanted to see him again.

Most nights, overcome by fatigue and yielding to a pleasant sense of satisfaction, Jai's sleep was a blackout. But that night, he was awakened twice. He was dreaming. Almost touching him there was a small silver lake, and in the centre of its surface there appeared a passionate-looking head, not quite human, and yet it reminded him of someone. Its eyes seemed to gleam sadly, but that, thought Jai, might have been the effect of the reflected silver of the lake. Then he noticed that sprouting from the top of the head was a cluster of beautiful fresh flowers. He started to walk round the lake, but it seemed to move to him, and when it touched him he woke up startled. Then he slept again and the lake was now moving rapidly away. The face again turned sadly to him. He ran toward it, but he stumbled, and just as he was about to identify the face, a great plant, like a tall full-grown stalk of corn with one bursting ripe cob on it, stood in the foreground. The plant began to wave its arms, beckoning to the lake, and the cob nodded. The plant touched his eyes and he awoke. He lay on his bed, wondering, but unable to find any acceptable meaning.

At last he slept again, feeling as though something had ripped through him and then shoved him aside.

CHAPTER SIX

SWARAJYA—a word denoting not so much the right as the obligation to rule oneself—became the motto of the people, given to them by Gandhi. He decided that he would test their understanding of this new urge. The British Government not only had a monopoly in the manufacture of salt in India, but taxed the salt that the common people ate and deliberately kept production down so that imports were necessary to meet the full requirements of the country. This was neither fair to the poor peasant of India, nor was it common sense; the country could save money by making its own salt instead of importing it. So Gandhi said that the people must ignore the laws and make the salt that they required for their own use. This was not to be done in secrecy, but openly; for, in making salt, the people would only be exercising an obvious right. Would the people be willing to go out and openly exercise their right? It would mean that they would be arrested by the police and sent to jail; they would have no defence, for they would be breaking the law. All this Gandhi was explaining to the whole country.

Then the news broke that Gandhi had informed the British Government that on the 12th of March, 1930, he would set out to walk the two hundred and forty-one miles from his ashram at Sabarmati, through the villages and towns to the sea at Dandi, where he would manufacture salt in defiance of the law. To the people Gandhi announced that when he reached Dandi, the whole nation was to join him in making salt. Thus the country—unarmed—was to match itself against the might of the British Government. When the leaders met at Shanti Devi's house to draw up plans for Delhi's salt-making, the place was soon surrounded by shopkeepers, tailors, landlords, sweepers, lawyers, railway workers, bank clerks, petty hawkers, tonga drivers, and teachers who had come to tell the leaders that the whole city, except some of the women and children, had decided to join in the salt-making. At this there was an outcry from the women, who asked whether the country was not just as much theirs as it was the men's.

Each day of Gandhi's march to Dandi became a new awakening for the people. It was as if suddenly they were walking along a high mountain ridge and could see the past receding into perspective on one side while the faint lines of a future of freedom stretched out to the far horizon on the other. And each day they trembled also with fear that the British Government would arrest their leader and cut off their hopes; but, for no reason that history can precisely discover, the British seemed from now on to act as if they, too, were being impelled to become part of the new drama of India. And so, to the amazement of all, the greatest march in the history of India continued uninterrupted.

Each day, tens of millions of people in the remote villages would hear of the march and feel their spirits rise into a sphere of freedom; and each day, by the hundred and by the thousand, the people of the villages and towns through which Gandhi walked, joined him for a portion of his journey and felt the quiet, reassuring, and peaceful presence of this smiling man, which forever remained with them.

CHAPTER SEVEN

PANDIT BRIJ KRISHEN, the great leader from Lucknow, had been at Shanti Devi's house for the meeting with the local leaders. When he returned to Dewan House, he was fuming.

"These people have no spirit and no ideas; only a great show of pious proprietorship in the success of the national movement," he said bitterly.

Of course, Pandit Brij Krishen conveniently overlooked the fact that he himself regarded the Movement as largely his own private show. No doubt he would concede that Gandhiji and a few others had shares in the company. This he felt was perfectly obvious. The selected few were the natural proprietors. As for the others, they were there to do with their lives, their money, and their time as they were told by the Big Leaders.

Most of the guests had already arrived when Dewan Ram Nath came in alone—his wife ignored these sociabilities. He beamed at Geeta, glad to see her with her friends. Anything that Geeta did was sure to be right, he thought. He completely trusted her instinct.

"Are our guests served with everything they want? Geeta, I hope you are all enjoying yourselves," he said. Then he sighed. "But these days I never know whether one asks young people that. They don't seem to want to enjoy themselves. Then, what do they want? Yes, what do you and your friends want, Geeta?" He begged her for an answer, his little pointed beard nodding rapidly half-way round the room.

Geeta was displaying her best party manners before her friends, and though rather bored at Ram Nath's question, she smiled at him coyly and said: "Why, Uncle, of course we want to enjoy ourselves, and just at this minute we are enjoying your hospitality."

And immediately there were little sounds of approval from all over the room echoing Geeta's words. The Dewan tugged at his little beard, very pleased with himself. Why weren't all his moments as happy as this one? It was so simple. Life was going sweetly on its own way. Geeta was quite right. And now she was saying something more to him: "Our generation is only adding a little bit to what you and your generation have given us. Don't you see that, Uncle?" and she smiled at him.

Yes, of course he saw that. He nodded his head several

times. But then, why were most people, including himself,
so afraid of the very thought of change? Out loud he said:
"So foolish, so foolish! Oh—not you, not you. It's we old
people who are so foolish not to realize what goes on before
our eyes. But tell me now, do you think we older people
have done you poorly—do you feel your heritage should have
been richer?" he asked.

"You've done us pretty well, Dewan Sahib," said one of
the young captains from the Rajputana Rifles, smiling very
broadly; and, looking at two young beauties from Calcutta,
he repeated: "Pretty well, pretty well." But no one seemed
to pay any attention to what he said.

It was to listen to Lena that they turned. She burst forth;
her face flushed and her eyes very bright: "Nothing has been
done for the women. It's appalling. We have to fight for
everything. I wonder sometimes what is going to happen
to us. Because we insist on our rights, we are going to become
terribly quarrelsome, and if we do, it will be you men who
will be to blame." She was very upset and her face, which
had been wonderfully radiant, turned cold and hard.

Ram Nath was all for taking up this challenge, and re-
joined: "Come, come, Lena, you, above all, to be saying this?
Your parents have provided you with all the opportunities
that we give our boys. How can you complain?" And he
looked at her as if pitying her for bursting out so uncontrol-
lably.

Lena said nothing. She was abashed at herself and aware
that all the young men were looking at her. She wondered
what they thought. But she tried to get her mind back on
her own plight, seeking secret justification for her outburst.
She thought of all the struggles that her mother had had
with her father over her education. It hadn't mattered to her,

in a way, but now she saw it as a great waste of effort. Not waste, really, because—well, the women were managing to get somewhere. She shook her head and then, finding she was on the right track again, she went on: "It is the wrong way of doing things. We women pay so heavily for our gains. We have to give up an inner treasure, a sort of sweetness which, if only we could keep, we would—well, we would be the sort of women we were meant to be." And she blushed.

Jai felt terribly uncomfortable listening to her, as though he himself were an obstacle to the life that Lena wanted to lead. Was he? He wanted to ask her. He wanted to know and to set this right.

Jai was going to say something, but at that moment he saw Pandit Brij Krishen entering the room and everyone rising to greet him. Jai thought Geeta's father looked very impressive. His features were inclined to be massive, but they were perfectly proportioned and the stern quality of his face did not entirely conceal a deeper kindliness. It was as though he had acquired the sternness because he thought he had to have it for certain occasions, but knew also when it was to be dispensed with. As usual with all the nationalist leaders, he was dressed in a white hand-woven cotton shirt and trousers to match, but over these simple clothes he wore the finest white Kashmiri shawl with a narrow edge of tapestry, like embroidery.

. He went around the room meeting all of them, his folded hands raised in a namaskar to the women, while at the men he directed a searching look. When he came to Jai, he remembered that he wanted specially to talk with him. Geeta looked to see what impression Jai was making and she thought her father looked pleased, but that was her imagina-

tion. Brij Krishen, in fact, formed no impression whatsoever
of Jai. All he did was to recollect that this was the man he
wanted to meet, and, with that, he remembered also the stu-
pidity of the leaders of Delhi. He sat down by Jai and, ad-
dressing the silence in the room, he said: "Why have all of
you stopped talking? If Ram Nath is young enough to be
allowed to listen, then you can't disqualify me. Let me
listen."

"Papa, Lena was just saying what a hard time women
have. She says we have to fight for everything in a man-
made world," explained Geeta.

"Extraordinary idea!" pronounced the great Pandit
instantaneously, as though he had just heard something that
had no right to have entered his hearing. Then he went on
in a quite different voice, as if trying to understand something about life. "Most people live as they happen to have
been born to live, and a few, for some reason that we can't
explain, try to do something new. Most of the time it is because the older sources of livelihood are crowded out and
something else must be found. Ram Nath, you ought to
know more about these things. You spend your time reading
about them. Hasn't the history of mankind been rather like
this?"

"Yes, yes, of course it has." Ram Nath did not have the
courage to disagree with the highly successful and respected
Brij Krishen. "The search for food and shelter, and complica-
tions arising out of the search—and, of course, human van-
ity; that's all there is, that's all."

Jai felt that it was going to be extremely difficult for him
to talk to the Pandit, and he began to hope that a general
conversation would develop, in which case he could keep

quiet. But that was not to be. Brij Krishen really was troubled about the state of affairs in Delhi, and he now addressed himself to Jai:

"Well, Jai Singh, the Movement in Delhi is in a hopeless state—no leadership, none at all!"

Jai struggled hard against a great reluctance to talk to this great man. But he realized that he had to say something, and he tried now to put briefly what he felt. "Panditji, the people will create their own leaders when the time comes. What they want from you is no more than some encouragement and confidence," he said.

"But I am doing that all the time. I have just been telling these things to your leaders. If they cannot convey them to the people, that is just too bad," replied the Pandit.

Jai did not want to say any more. There was no need, for the people were by no means indifferent to the Movement and, whatever Brij Krishen or the local leaders might do or say, the people would do as Gandhi and Nehru, and perhaps a handful of others, would tell them.

Even Ram Nath was surprised at Brij Krishen's attitude. "But, Brij Krishen, don't you know that, before the British, our own rulers, even the worst of them, themselves went to the people at times of crisis and told them directly what to do? Even the Imperial Moghuls did that. Then, why can't you meet the people and tell them yourself what you want of them instead of speaking through their so-called half-witted leaders?" he asked.

Brij Krishen turned his massive face to Ram Nath and looked at him for half a minute as if unable to believe that these words could have come from him. Not because anything brilliant had been said—on the contrary, he felt certain that nothing brilliant could be said by Ram Nath. What surprised him was that this perfectly obvious remark did, in fact, contain the sum and substance of the problem posed by the situation in Delhi. But he wasn't going to admit it. So he turned his face away from Ram Nath and said: "That is perfectly obvious, my dear Ram Nath. Indeed, that is what this young man and I have just agreed about. Jai Singh, thank you for telling me what you think. You should keep me in touch with developments here. And now, all of you," he said, turning to Geeta, "must excuse me, and return to your party mood."

They all rose, and he made a salutation as he left the room; only Ram Nath looked the other way, hurt by the insult that Brij Krishen had administered to him. He didn't know that, in the estimation of the young people in the room, he had in fact come off very well for having told the leader how to go about his business. He sighed, and after wondering for a moment whether it would be in keeping with his dignity to retire to his own room, he glanced at Geeta and decided to spend some time talking to her. He went toward her, looking very crestfallen, but she beamed at him both because she was glad that he had talked like that to her father and because she knew he was hurt and she wanted to make amends for Brij Krishen's rudeness.

Lena came up to him and said: "Dewan Ram Nath, thank you for telling Pandit Brij Krishen that. You have helped the Movement in Delhi more than any of the leaders in this city. It was wonderful."

Ram Nath suddenly became aware of the general approval of the room, and his despondency and sense of injury lifted. "It was nothing, nothing," he said. "It is all so obvious. Of course, I am an administrator. I know about these things. Our politicians have had no experience, but they will learn," and he felt very pleased at his patronizing statement about the great leader.

Just then, a servant came in and told Ram Nath that Raja Muzaffar Khan had arrived. The Dewan got up immediately and rushed toward the door, thinking of his last encounter with the devilish old Raja. He was hurrying not out of politeness, but because he did not want the Raja to come into the room and meet these sweet young people. He feared that Muzaffar might even say something about their visit to Ranu at Adampur. But the young people knew nothing about these rather panicky thoughts in Ram Nath's mind. To them it seemed that he was just being specially polite and cringing to a social superior. This conduct horrified them and Ram Nath immediately fell from the pedestal he had won for himself in his encounter with Brij Krishen. The young people felt again an alienness from the older generation.

Jai decided that this moment of preoccupation with a new and important guest gave him an opportunity to leave. He wanted to rush out of the room.

He went up to Geeta to make his apologies. She was talking to the stiff young Indian administrator and matching his anglicisms with a kind of improvised sophistication. She was aware that Jai wished to leave, but, perversely, she tried to draw him into the conversation. She thought she could impress and interest him by holding her own against the snobbish administrator. But Jai remained aloof till Geeta, disengaging herself, came up to him.

"I am glad you talked to my father. He meets so few

people who are capable of conversing with him, you know," and her tone and expression gave him the feeling that he had been permitted to tread on a velvet carpet from Merz.

Jai replied quickly, but with a smile: "Of course, it takes two to make conversation. But I suppose he is generally too preoccupied to make the effort."

Geeta was taken aback that he should turn her point round on her, and she raised her eyebrows as if to deliver a rhetorical question. But quickly she changed her mind, deciding not to provoke Jai further. In an icy, clipped voice, she remarked: "That is a plebeian theory, my dear Jai."

And because Jai did not respond immediately, she deemed herself the victor. Magnanimously holding out her hand to him, she said with a smile, her face flushed with excitement: "Come, we are going to dance. I will teach you. Don't leave just yet." Her eyes were very bright and she poised her head to one side as if to coax him to accept her invitation.

"It is very kind of you," said Jai, bowing slightly. "But perhaps some other time."

Geeta shrugged her shoulders, and, her lips thin and inflexible, she replied: "Just as you like, my dear Jai. But with my friends it is I who pick the moments. I think you will find that that is so," and she nodded at him stiffly before turning on her heel and walking away.

Glad to be relieved of her presence, and not wanting to risk another chance meeting with her, Jai waved to Shabir and, ignoring the others, walked rapidly out of the room.

Jai felt that he wanted to leave forever—leave the atmosphere that was developing in this group and among the leaders who were supposed to direct them. As he walked out of the gate of Dewan House, he thought of the hills and of the valley beyond the mountain home of his family where he had spent all the summers of his childhood and youth. Out of this Delhi afternoon, he stepped into that valley and looked up at the great Himalayas standing over him. They seemed to come nearer, even to touch him, but he dared not disturb them in their quietness as they watched—the roof of the world, watching over the great plains of India.

Jai felt the mountains as a benison over him, and the sorrow that had filled him seemed to fall away. He felt now that his hostility toward his friends had been unreasonable. Why should he be upset by Geeta or by her father? What about his own feeling for Lena or for Shabir? Did he always behave with them as he wanted to? Jai smiled at himself. He ought to go back and apologize for his behaviour, but he couldn't quite face that. Slowly he walked toward New Delhi, the city that the British had just built to be the capital of their Indian Empire.

He wondered how, at one time and one place, there could simultaneously flourish a deep human faith in two opposing ideas. Here were the British with their faith strong enough in their own destiny in India to build a new and magnificent habitation for themselves. When they heard people around them saying that all foreign conquerors who built themselves a new city at Delhi were really building a lavish mausoleum for their unwanted power, they laughed and said openly that it was absurd to liken them to the barbarian conquerors of the past. Were they not the leaders of the world in science, and had they not developed weapons so deadly that unarmed men could be mown down by the thousand? Surely, then, their power would endure for countless time to come.

The opposing faith was that of the people. They were learning again the recorded steps of their own traditions and the meaning of the onward flow of life which was again to sweep over this ancient area of the world. They felt certain that very soon they would pick up the neglected threads of life against which exterior forces would be helpless.

Jai gazed out to the south and saw the broken line of the old fort of Indraprastha against the sky. It was there, through the ages, that the contestants for the mastery of this gateway to the full depth of India had erected their fortifications, proclaiming their strength and their determination to stay at the helm of affairs; but none had succeeded. Why had not India gone on from the wonderful experiments of Asoka, or of Chandragupta Vikramaditya, or of Harsha; or of Akbar, who had seen the folly of foreign rule in India and had taken the best in Hindu, Buddhist, Christian, and Moslem thinking, basing his system of administration on the tradition of the country and giving the highest offices to the sons of the soil? Many of these experiments had seemed to take deep root— but since the time of Akbar, the good periods had become like brief tricks conjured up by some great magician to divert the crowd for a moment or two. Was the present reawakening no more than the masterful achievement of the great magician Gandhi, or was it also a deep realization among the people that for too long they had forgotten their heritage as human beings?

The setting sun was being received by a low screen of clouds, and the whole bowl of the sky was now a great violet quietness in which all questions seemed to melt away. Jai stood and let the quietness overtake him. His tensions eased. The peace of the evening surged through him, and he felt the stillness that had come upon him as part of the vast calm that touched the far sweetness of the violet sky and throbbed also in the quiet earth on which he stood.

CHAPTER EIGHT

GEETA RESENTED Jai's departure, but thought too well of herself to display her feelings. Turning to the room, gaily she said: "Now that the bores have left, let us dance." In the silence that greeted this very bold suggestion, she lit a cigarette and added: "Then we can go on to a cinema."

A phonograph played the latest Hollywood melodies and then they danced. The girls from Calcutta, the Captain, and his friend in the Administration were experts, and Geeta and Lena, too, danced well. The others were beginners.

In the Dewan's private sitting-room, Muzaffar Khan was making enticing suggestions to Ram Nath. Coaxingly, his face pleasantly flushed, he said: "Come, my dear friend, let us go to Adampur. Ranu now has a companion—both of them are girls from Paradise, so lovely. You will feel much better."

Ram Nath had promised himself that never again would he visit Adampur, but, hearing of the new situation there in which he would not be so utterly neglected, he was beginning to weaken. He couldn't think of a single good reason to refuse. Nevertheless, his face looking very grave, he said: "No, no, Raja Sahib. Those visits are not for me."

But Muzaffar Khan only laughed and, twirling his moustache, asked: "And how are you any different from me?"

Ram Nath thought of his own more serious pursuits and looked furtively at the rows of books against the walls, but at this moment they all seemed entirely irrelevant and trifling. He smiled, and they were about to leave together when the sound of the dance music came from the drawing-room. It caught Muzaffar Khan's ear and, cocking his head to one side, he proclaimed: "But, Ram Nath, this sounds like the music at Davico's, where the British and their friends dance. Why didn't you tell me of this gaiety? Let us go and see, and join in. Yes, let us learn these modern fashions: I believe in being fashionable. Come, come." And he started to move off.

Ram Nath was very nervous. He followed his guest with bated breath. What was going on? It must be the doing of that stupid Captain, he thought. Never, never again would he set foot in this house, swore Ram Nath to himself.

When the two friends reached the drawing-room, the dancing was in full swing. The Raja was all smiles and his eyes darted happily in all directions. Seeing this, Ram Nath foresaw the worst and was at once afraid and furious. Muzaffar saw one of the girls from Calcutta sitting out. He went up to her and, bowing charmingly, sat down beside her.

"I am Raja Muzaffar Khan," he said with great self-assurance, and then immediately his Old World manners prompted him to give her a worthy place by his side, so he continued: "and I am honoured to sit next to so beautiful a lady whose grace and charm fill this room with sweetness."

The girl from Calcutta smiled and hoped that someone would come and ask her to dance. Muzaffar Khan seemed to sense the danger of losing her, so he acted quickly.

"Please, dear lady, do teach me to dance," and he got up and bowed.

She was somewhat awed by this aging feudal character, but soon found him full of alacrity and rhythm. Muzaffar Khan regarded this as another entertainment that life, in its bounty, was providing. Perfectly relaxed, he thoroughly enjoyed himself shuffling across the floor.

Poor Ram Nath was neither feudal enough to look upon life the way his friend did, nor westernized enough to accept the naturalness of this form of relaxation. When Geeta saw his displeasure, she came up to him and said: "Come, Uncle, dance with me."

Ram Nath was speechless and his face turned as grey and splintery as his beard. Could she mean this? He looked around the room to see whether any of the others thought, as he did, that he was being insulted. But no one seemed to be paying any attention whatsoever except the Raja, who was gaily beckoning to him as much as to say: "Come on, dance, you old fool! Look what I have got." And gloating over his pretty young partner, Muzaffar Khan manœuvred along, half leading and half stumbling over her.

The poor Dewan looked beseechingly at Geeta. Why didn't she explain how his stately drawing-room had come to be transformed into a dancing-hall? And how could she ask him to dance? Couldn't she see that he could not behave like that shameless old scoundrel Muzaffar Khan?

Geeta saw his perplexity and realized that soon he would

be terribly hurt unless she saved him from the confusion which he was working up in himself. She took him to the far corner of the room and explained: "It was I who suggested that we should dance because it is such good exercise and such good fun. You know, I learned it at school in Switzerland."

He looked at her incredulously, and then spluttered: "At school with your girl friends, yes, and in Switzerland—but how can you compare that with this?" And he looked across at the Raja and at the young Captain, who was dancing with his eyes practically closed and had not even noticed the entry of the Dewan.

Geeta tried again. "Uncle, do not fret yourself," she said. "No one will come to any harm, not even the girl dancing with the Raja. She has danced in Calcutta with scores of Rajas. You must trust me to see that nothing happens that would even remotely disgrace you," and she looked at him deeply with her large eyes.

He pressed her hand and made a movement with his lower lip which sometimes came involuntarily when he felt that he had established his point. In this instance, Geeta rightly intrepreted it to mean that he had accepted her point, so she rose from his side, whispering: "Anyway, we will soon be stopping." And she returned to the dance floor.

But Geeta was reckoning without the Raja. He was in a transport of delight and was not planning to stop for a long time to come. As the senior guest in the house and as an old friend of the Dewan's, his wishes would have to come first. A slow fox-trot had just been smudged out by the heavy grooves at the end of the record, but the Raja was still dancing. His partner skillfully disentangled herself, and then he came to.

Meanwhile, the Captain had started to clap and to call: "Hear, hear!"

Muzaffar Khan now caught the idea and, clapping his large fat hands, he said: "Yes, Captain, yes, that's the spirit —'hear, hear!' Of course. This is the most wonderful dance in the world. I must teach it to all my friends. Therefore, I must learn it better. Please let us go on with the dance. Ram Nath—" He looked commandingly at the Dewan. Ram Nath turned helplessly to Geeta.

Another record was put on, and again Muzaffar Khan danced with the girl from Calcutta, whom he was now calling "Cuckoo," as one would a pretty young child. He was not really thinking of her any more. The dance had transported him beyond the confines of the room. He was thinking of Ranu—how wonderfully she sang and danced. Now he would teach her this dance, so that they could embrace and glide together—and he almost swooned with delight at the sensuous crescendo of his own thought.

His mind leaped forward with its fantasy. Instantly he would take this party to Adampur. Ranu would sit behind the lattice on the roof; she was so quick and graceful that at once she would learn these dances, and then what delight he would have with her.

The music stopped, and now the Raja knew that meant he must stop dancing; besides, he was to take the party to his estate.

"Ram Nath, it is very warm here, don't you think?" he said. "Let us all go and dance in the cool garden at Adampur. Do come, all of you are welcome. I will send for my other car."

The Dewan could not believe it. How could the old fool suggest such a thing? Imagine taking these respectable young people to the place where he kept his women! Would he now try to get one of these young girls to remain with him for the night? That must be his game, decided Ram Nath, and his heart was pounding with rage.

Poor Ram Nath. There was another cause for his misery and confusion. He had been hoping that after the dance he could slip away with Muzaffar Khan to the estate and meet Ranu's companion. Now the Raja had made that impossible.

"Raja Muzaffar Khan, we are expecting people to dinner. We would be honoured to visit your estate, but I must beg you to excuse us," said Ram Nath with great dignity.

The Raja's response was to laugh good-naturedly and to say: "Ram Nath, you know best; but I thought you, in any case, had accepted my invitation for the evening. Don't you think you should keep your word to an old friend? But please yourself. Really, we must not stand on formalities. I can see that the young people are coming with me." And turning to them, he added: "Come, let us go."

All of them left except Lena, who did not join the Raja's party but went home in her own car. Ram Nath felt his clotted rage fizzle into a heavy, inert depression. He went to his room to try to re-establish some calm. Could one never, never go quietly away and be thoroughly relaxed?—he was rationalizing his desire to go to Adampur. Couldn't one depend on anyone?—the Raja was the test case. Why, then, couldn't he find enough satisfaction here?—and he looked around at his books and the heavy leather-covered chairs. He sighed, trying to resign himself to the situation.

That evening, after many months, Ram Nath was very gentle with his wife. But he slept badly. It was to Adampur that his confused mind kept taking his body.

CHAPTER NINE

CAME THE DAY when Gandhi halted five miles from the sea-coast and told the people of India and the British Government that the next morning he would take water from the sea and evaporate it till the salt that God had put into it remained, and the salt would be distributed freely among the poor instead of being taxed as had been decreed by the Government. He invited the whole country to join with him in making salt.

That night all Delhi was filled with the excitement of preparation for salt-making. The leaders met hastily at the home of Shanti Devi to consider how they could fulfil the wish of Gandhiji. Lena managed to creep into the meeting-room, for she simply had to hear what would be said in this momentous discussion. She trembled with excitement. No one knew what would happen the next day. Perhaps, thought Lena, the foreign ruler would become like an enraged demon in the old story-books and crush the people. On the other hand—and her excitement rose to an extreme pitch as she thought of this—perhaps the British would go to Gandhiji tomorrow and ask him to take over the Government and then she and all the people could begin the actual remaking of their beloved India.

The leaders made their decision. Early next morning they would go, in procession with the people, to the banks of the River Jamuna and take water from the river which, on evaporation, would leave a residue of salt. They were well pleased with the scheme, and, in coming to this solemn resolve, no one remembered that the fresh water of the river simply did not contain any salt.

Word of the plan spread quickly all about the city. From every house came the clatter of pots and pans in the search for the very brightest utensils to be used in the important ceremony of the morrow. Gay charcoal-burners were chosen and little bundles of charcoal prepared for extracting non-existent salt from the river.

All the men of Delhi except those working in Government offices, most of them accompanied by their womenfolk and children, stepped out in the eager morning air on the great exodus to the river. As they went on their way, they chanted the names of Ram and Allah and Gandhi.

The authorities were completely taken aback by the move. It had never occurred to them that the whole city would decide to go to the river to make salt. Some of the high officials in the hierarchy said this was indeed a brilliant stroke and they attributed it to the evil genius of Gandhi: they were sure that somehow he had managed to send an emissary to the local leaders conveying this idea! Now it was the turn of the governors to confer hastily. And in their momentous conference it no more struck these tried administrators that river water could yield no salt than it had occurred to the leaders of the people. If only this obvious fact had dawned on them, they could have poured ridicule on the plan of the leaders simply by announcing it all over the city. If, after the scientific position had been made clear, the people went on with their chimera, the rulers could have proclaimed that no action would be taken under the law, as in fact the salt law could not be broken by an attempt to make salt from river water.

But the drama of peoples, no less than love, often closes its eyes completely to the facts. Certainly these simple facts about salt were lost sight of in thousands of towns and cities in India where the people thought they were breaking the salt laws.

The police, strengthened by units from an infantry brigade at the Cantonment, cordoned off the river from the city. An order prohibiting the manufacture of salt from the waters of the river was hastily drafted in the incomprehensible language of the law books and proclaimed from scores of points in Delhi, accompanied by beat of drum.

The authorities felt secure after the proclamation and took up their positions with the cordon of armed police and troops. But some of the leaders and a few of the townsfolk who had left for the river very early in the morning had already got there before these steps had been taken. However, the main surge of the population of the city going toward the river found itself suddenly facing the line of rather confused armed men blocking its way.

Lena and her mother were among the early group that had got to the river. There they had eagerly taken water and boiled it on their charcoal braziers till it burned away. What little sand and dust remained in their pots they triumphantly scraped together. Shabir and Lena and some of the others tasted it and pronounced it definitely to be salt. There were nods, smiles, and words of congratulation all around. Thus was Gandhiji's injunction obeyed, and the law was thought to have been well and truly broken. With great solemnity, little portions of the scrapings were put on small pieces of coloured paper and neatly wrapped like powders dispensed by a chemist. They were then tucked away in the women's handbags to be taken safely back to the city.

As they approached the outskirts of Delhi, they saw the great marching crowds, dressed in gay festive colours, held back by the police. They advanced toward the cordon. On seeing the small group approaching from the river, the police were thrown into a state of complete perplexity. Their instructions were to keep the people from going to the river, but they had not been told what to do about people returning from the river. As the leaders came in sight, they were greeted by the crowds with loud shouts of "Victory to Gandhi!" Those who were in the front rows shouted questions:

"Have you brought us some salt?"

"Have you carried out Gandhiji's instructions?"

Shabir shouted back: "Yes, friends, we have made salt and are bringing it back to the city."

The crowd was mad with joy at this news, and shouts of "Victory to Gandhi!" roared into the sky, while thousands added to the din by clattering the pots and pans they were carrying to the river.

As the reverberations of the shouting and the roar reached the ears of the top British administrators sitting in New Delhi, they decided that this was surely the call for a mass rising against them. Manfully they rose to meet the situation as they imagined it. They collected their womenfolk and children in the stately palace of the Viceroy and they vowed to save the Empire from disintegration. Immediate orders were issued to the military and police commanders to disperse the "mob."

Again the facts were completely lost sight of so that history might move on. The shouting of the people was no more than the joyful consummation of their imagined act of law-breaking. Most of them were anxious now to return home and to get on with the daily tasks of life; soon their enthusiasm would have dropped a little, and perhaps that would have been as far as this particular scene in the drama would have gone. But the great awakening of the people and their movement to freedom was to sweep further forward irrespective of the logic of the immediate events.

During the shouting, Jai, who was among those held up by the armed cordon, had caught Lena's eye. She had smiled warmly at him, and he was very glad that she had been among those to reach the river. She, too, was happy and pleased to see him. In the pandemonium, he was as calm as if he knew what all this was about. His quiet strength in the face of the terrifying situation in which armed men separated them imparted to Lena a sense of calmness.

Lena and Jai again were smiling at each other when the police captain, in obedience to the order from the Imperial rulers at New Delhi, blew his whistle and one of his lieutenants proclaimed that the people must forthwith disperse or face the consequences. The people knew what was implied in the ominous phrase "or face the consequences," and they looked across the cordon to their leaders, waiting for guidance.

For a few moments the leaders pondered, and then they called out: "People of Delhi, remain peacefully where you are!"

This was too much for the authorities, who, without waiting, ordered the police to charge the crowd. The townsfolk were by no means all heroes. And when the police charged, swinging their heavy clubs, and the military used the butt ends of their rifles, many ran for their lives, taking their children and women with them, and they were glad to reach the deserted city streets and quickly enter their homes. But a surprisingly large number, tens of thousands, refused to leave.

The police wondered whether they should be striking at these unarmed and helpless men and women, but they were men of discipline, and so they continued to hit out while the injured fell or limped about in large numbers. Jai was hit twice—once on his arm when he raised it to shield his head, and then across the chest. He felt numbed by the pain and yet terribly roused by the indignity of the situation. He stood his ground, and the wave of police passed beyond him into the crowd. Lena rushed up to him. Jai was concerned for her, and, taking her arm with his sound one, he led her back toward Shanti Devi and the group of leaders.

"Please take care of yourself," he begged, "and don't let them hurt you." He felt that if the police were to strike her, he would not be able to hold himself in check. When they reached her mother, he said: "I must go and tend those who are badly hurt. I will bring them here to you."

"But you yourself are badly hurt, Jai," pleaded Lena. "Do not go. You must not." And she tore a strip from the end of her sari and made Jai wait while she bandaged his arm.

His chest was hardening into a great lump of pure pain, but he said nothing about it. He felt better as she wound the bandage about his arm, wondering at her deftness and at the great tenderness that rose up in him.

He wanted to take Lena in his arms, but he was aware again of the situation around him—the people were groaning or quietly nursing their wounds, and the police were tiring of their wretched occupation and were letting the people stand about or get away as they wished. The unforeseeable had happened. For the present, at any rate, the authorities had had a surfeit of force and many of the city folk had stood their ground and taken physical punishment without flinching. Neither side knew what step it should take next.

Jai went up to the wounded. Among them was Munshi Ram, the wealthy landlord—he had been severely beaten— and Gafoor, a cousin of Shabir's, whose head was bleeding. Munshi Ram's relatives were bringing a stretcher to him. Jai helped Gafoor back to Lena, Shabir, and the others. They bound his head, and two of them assisted him to walk.

They started now to move toward the city. Seeing Jai and Gafoor bandaged, a zealous policeman came up to them as if to attack them again. At this point Shanti Devi, elderly and portly though she was, took command of the situation. She strode rapidly to the front and dared the man to strike her or her party. The man stopped short, and as he heard her words his hardened face seemed to disintegrate as though the sap were flowing out of him. He turned and darted away to one side.

Finally they reached a car belonging to one of the party. Jai could walk no longer, and even in the car he felt that he could scarcely breathe. They took him to a friendly doctor—a leading man in his profession who, though he served at the Government hospital, treated without charge those engaged in the Freedom Movement.

Two of Jai's ribs were fractured. The doctor set them and prepared a plaster, but agreed that Jai need not remain too long in bed provided he did not strain himself or again put himself at the mercy of the iron-shod staves of the police.

CHAPTER TEN

THAT NIGHT the pain took autonomous possession of Jai. He felt it goad him from one side of his bed to the other and back again. It flung his arms and legs about, and as his fever rose, he felt his broken rib gore through his nose into the marrow of his brain, while the other fractured bone seemed to be gouging out his eye. With his other eye and with his injured arm and the back of his hand, he fought the pain in a delirium of fever.

In the morning he was still delirious, and when Shabir

came in, he was talking in the intensity of his unresolved struggle:

"Fan the coals, bright coal burning, don't burn away the salt, salt in the fire now, taste the bright white coal. Fan harder, white coal is salt. Lena don't touch it, so tenderly you touch and smile, so tenderly; the coal will keep its white saltiness now, no grey ashes. Salt in the ashes too. . . . Shanti Devi, mother of salt, no, mother of Lena who makes salt and frees me. Lena made salt to free me, but don't, not salt, not salt, that hurts now, burning me, yes, the white coal; Lena, smile at the salt, smile softly at the coal—salt turning to white smooth crystal rock, cool against this split eye . . . smooth salt rock, the salt is free! Free! But the people! Lena, don't look so sad. Your eyes have seen my hurt and the people. See my other eye, my bright and smiling eye and this arm, to win me back from the hurt, yes, win me back. . . ."

Shabir ran and fetched the doctor. Jai was still tossing in his bed, and the muttered words came from his lips. Then he grew silent, his jaws tightly clenched. The doctor gave him an injection of morphine and he slept heavily that whole day and the next night.

The third day, early, Jai felt the chirping of the birds against his skin. The soles of his feet were tranquil and thoughtful, and his arm gazed out at the cool morning light. The other arm, the injured one, was still asleep, as was the upper part of his torso in its casing of plaster. He let them sleep, keeping his mind from turning to them, and with the rest of himself he communed delightedly with the early-morning freshness.

Eyes filled with the cool greenness of the peepul trees, his mind went tumbling over the leaves to range across the quiet city to the large mansion on Rajpura Road where Lena lived with her parents. Was she, too, sensing this exquisite morning? He wished he could get up and run to her house and walk with her on the romantic, rocky, copper-coloured ridge that stood over the outskirts of Delhi. He smiled at the idea, wondering how Pandit Dharma Das would react to his taking out the beautiful Lena. What, her father would say, would the other respectable Brahmin households think of his daughter—so beautiful and obviously very marriageable —if they saw her out in the early morning with a young Rajput? Of course, in the older and freer days of India, Lena could have set at rest any chance of gossip by placing a garland of flowers on his neck, and then he would have been her chosen groom.

Jai turned off these fancies. More fully awake, he was troubled by the feeling that remained after the salt-making. He was not sure that anything had been achieved. And what if the people were too timid to make another effort? He felt terribly isolated and without any warmth or gladness. Why, indeed, had he taken all this so seriously? Of course no salt had been made and no laws had been broken. Was it all just a farce? And though thousands of the city folk had stood their ground, had not far too many been beaten back by the police and the army? What part had he played in all this? He could remember only Lena, only see her smile across the police cordon. All of the rest was confusing, and it filled him with despair.

Worried by these thoughts, Jai dozed again. When he awoke, he was overcome with confusion. Lena was in his room. It was not till several moments later that he saw Shabir also and two or three other workers. They had brought him fruit and nuts, and all of them looked elated. What had happened?

Shabir smiled at him and Lena looked very lovely. He wished she had brought that garland for him to make his fantasies come true. He smiled back at his friends.

Shabir took his hand. "At last you are smiling and feel much better. Poor Jai. You know, there are about three hundred injured, at least twenty very seriously!"

Jai felt very well. His pains had gone. "Are the injured being properly cared for and fed?" he asked.

"Yes, yes," replied Lena. "Everyone in the city wants to help—especially those who ran away."

Shabir's face had grown rather serious, and Jai looked at him, expecting some explanation.

"They have arrested Jawaharlal and most of the other leaders. In all the provinces and cities people are being arrested by the thousands," said Shabir.

Jai glanced quickly at all of them. There was an unspoken strength among them. He felt his earlier depression shuffle off. They talked and made plans while they ate the nuts and fruit.

After an hour Jai was tired again and lay quietly. He heard their voices dimly like birds' wings flying near him, then silence. When he awoke, Lena was sitting on a hard office chair by his bed, reading.

She seemed to become aware of his open eyes and turned toward him. Smiling, she said: "We thought someone should remain till you were awake, to ask you what you needed," and her smile continued like an overflow from her words.

This was many stages ahead of his fantasy of walking with

her on the Ridge. So the fantasy had in a sense been real and already it was in the past. Jai was conscious of something surging ahead of even the daring of his dreams.

He looked at her. She was extraordinarily beautiful to him. Softly he called her name: "Lena." He was calling both to himself and to her. He felt her name touch everything in him and bring his whole self to a glowing liveness; and then the name he had called seemed to go out again from every fibre in him, not just to her senses but to every fibre in her. Never before had he known this kind of communication. It was more intense even than the first experience of beauty which had filled him one day in the mountains when he was about sixteen and became aware of the separate and exquisite liveness of a tree against the sky. Now he felt not just the impact of beauty but a constantly growing thing surging through him again and again. He wondered how strong it would become and what it would do to him.

Lena, too, was magnetized by hearing him call her name with such precise gentleness. Life seemed to be taking her, too, and sweeping her forward. She went to him and sat on his bed. He drew her to himself with his uninjured arm and held her warmth to his body. But that was not enough for her. She wanted to put her head close to his heart and feel the deep beat of his life. She did that, and a new surge swarmed up in her. She drew her whole body to his and held him to herself. His good arm tightened about her, and his mouth searched for her lips.

They lay there without any count of time. Then, prompted by another wave of care for him, she remembered that he was weak. She drew away a little and asked him softly whether he was in pain. He shook his head, but his face winced as the bruised body felt again the aches that came back into place as the tension in him unwound.

She soothed his chest with her hands. Tiredness filled him and he lay back quietly. She stood up to leave. For a moment he looked at her and felt his eyes take over the whole of himself; speech, touch, hunger, tenderness—all seemed to meet her in that one look. He knew that even if he shut his eyes, he would be intensely aware of her. It was as though he had only just learned what was meant by himself, by the person that was Jai Singh. His eyes were closing now, and he saw her smile and turn to go to the door.

Lena needed time to herself, so she walked. What had she done? What would her parents think? These questions and an uncertainty about the meaning of her new experience filled her with alarm. She tried to find some calm, and then the issues themselves seemed trivial and superficial. She was pervaded now by a feeling of relationship—she felt Jai all over her mind and body; she felt him as if she were almost he. She was two people now. And it was in this curious state that she turned into the gate of her home on Rajpura Road.

Entering the drawing-room, she came upon her parents in excited conversation. Her father was standing with his white Kashmiri shawl drawn tightly around him, his face flushed and imperious. She heard him say: ". . . that is all you care about her." As he said this, he saw Lena enter the room, and quickly he turned away as though his words had boomeranged and struck him in the face. Lena passed rapidly through the room, but could not resist the temptation to stand by her half-open door and listen.

Her father resumed: "Without any further delay, the girl must be found a husband."

"But how can we find a husband for a girl who refuses to be a wife?" asked Shanti Devi.

Pandit Dharma Das looked at his wife with angry contempt. "Refuses to be a wife!" he said. "That's impossible, and sheer nonsense. How can she refuse when the whole world thinks she ought to get married? It's just rubbish."

"Panditji, why go on like this? You know perfectly well that Lena doesn't think the world is concerned about her marriage; and besides, if she did think that, she would oppose the idea all the more strongly. Why don't you leave the girl in peace? Soon she will want a husband and then your wish will be fulfilled."

"All right, all right, Shanti Devi. I suppose you are right; but I warn you, you are taking a risk. And I beg of you not to engage me in these long, unseemly discussions. Really, what are we coming to?" And off went the Panditji to look at some of his briefs for the next day's work at the High Court. He was in the right mood now for work—his closing words had rewarded him with a pleasant feeling of virtuousness, and he had conveniently forgotten that it was he who had raised the topic, and that his wife generally avoided discussing these matters with him.

When her husband left, Shanti Devi sighed. She, too, would have liked Lena to find a husband. She knew that she was taking a risk. Her wealthy lawyer husband, to whom worldly success was a sacred duty, was right on this point. And she, Shanti Devi, had made things difficult for Lena by bringing her up in an unorthodox way. The girl would not hear of an arranged marriage—certainly not at present. And, in any case, all the parents who wanted that sort of marriage for their sons would regard her as likely to disrupt the traditional type of home, and rule her out. Shanti Devi wished that Lena could meet some of the fine young men of her own generation and from among them choose a husband. But alas, she reflected, only the seasoned national leaders came to the house. The young men stayed away, probably because they felt awed by her distinguished and successful husband, who was known to disapprove of his wife's new-fangled ideas.

At the end of the argument in the sitting-room, Lena shut the door and smiled to herself. She was pleased that she had become so important to her parents, and she was even more pleased because she had a secret in her heart, one that would make it unnecessary for them to worry over her. She thought of Jai, and a warm blush tingled through her.

That night, at dinner, Dharma Das saw a special kind of glow on his daughter's face. He was vaguely aware that it might be related to what she had overheard earlier in the evening when she had walked into the sitting-room. He felt slightly ashamed of himself and, consequently, he tried not to notice Lena.

CHAPTER ELEVEN

DEWAN RAM NATH entirely agreed with those who said that the Congress Party was making a foolish mistake in embarking on the crucial phase of the national movement on the basis of the disruption of the salt laws. The law, after all, was not something to be treated lightly, and the people should not be taught to bring it into contempt.

But no one in the country liked the salt laws, and many people hoped that a way out could be found which would save face all around. Accordingly, the Liberal Party, which consisted of the relatively better-educated feudal landlords and those leaders in the professions who had found favour with the British, very respectfully petitioned the Government to introduce a bill to rescind the salt tax; but the British unceremoniously told the Indian liberals to shut up.

Although Ram Nath regarded himself as far superior to the kind of people who joined the Liberal Party, he was peeved at its rebuff by the British. But he continued to think of the Congress as very stupid and of himself as one of the far-seeing wise few whom the country particularly needed at this time. How was he to express his wisdom?

He decided to give the Narain Das College one hundred thousand rupees for its Department of Government. But, of course, he could not just hand the money over to the college without the significance of the gift being made very clear. He accordingly told his secretary to invite the head of the college and the president of the governing body to come and see him. These worthy men wondered why Dewan Ram Nath was doing them this honour. Anyway, they attired themselves in their best long coats and presented themselves at the appointed time.

For the first hour or so they were given no hint of the reason for their presence at Dewan House. Indeed, their host spent most of the time talking to one of his managers, and virtually ignored them. The truth was that Ram Nath expected them to be fairly obsequious and he hoped they would refer with deference to the generosity of his father, who thirty years earlier had given the college a modest sum of money toward the cost of a hostel for the students; that would give him a suitable opening for what he wanted to say. But neither of the guests could possibly be aware of what was in his mind. How could they be? The hostel had long ago been sold because a neighbouring street had come to be inhabited by dancing girls and it was found that this distracting allurement was keeping the young men from their books.

Tired of waiting for his guests to open on the obvious note of previous generosity by his family, Ram Nath came testily to the point himself:

"Gentlemen, there is in these days an utter lack of appreciation of the real nature and true purpose of the art of government. I mean no disrespect to our great leaders, but are they not playing with fire in teaching the people to disobey the laws?" He looked at them searchingly.

The head of the college, a mild-looking plump man with a grey walrus moustache, was a staunch supporter of the Congress and, though he suspected he was being unwise, he could not refrain from defending its position. In a very quiet voice, he said: "But, Dewanji, might I remind your good self that in our country the people do not make the laws, and that they are equally powerless to alter them. Then, how can they have much respect for these laws?"

Ram Nath brushed this aside. His eyes flashed annoyance and he jutted his pointed grey beard at his visitors. "Do you gentlemen contest that there is a great need to understand these matters much better? As academic men, do you not want to advance the study of the theory of government?"

The men from the college were silent because they were too respectful to continue the argument. Ram Nath's look softened. He interpreted the silence as indicating agreement with what he had so wisely and clearly enunciated. With elation, he rushed ahead with his plan. He bent forward in his chair and, smiling victoriously, said: "Correct. You gentlemen are quite right. There is obviously a great need to reinforce these essential studies. I agree with you. The thing to do is to tell the misguided people of our city about this need and to announce to them—"

At this point the college president saw real danger ahead. No one in the city would listen to a theory that was so patently opposed to what Gandhiji was practising; in fact, the young men might refuse to come to a college which openly challenged the basis of the Freedom Movement, and that would mean the end of his own job. So he broke in, hoping to rescue the course of events from this fatal turn.

"Dewan Sahib, we are academic people. We are willing to study these matters, but we cannot be connected with any announcements to the people. We beg you to excuse us." And he looked as if he were about to leave.

Ram Nath's face flushed with anger. Raising his voice to a pitch of great irritation, he said: "Gentlemen, you must at least let me finish what I am trying to say. If you do not want any announcements, let us have a meeting at which I will speak and you will announce that I am giving the college a hundred thousand rupees to expand your Department of Government."

Half-way through this news, the college president felt very uncomfortable because the Dewan was well known for his extremely boring speeches. His orations were always interminable and his gestures so eccentric that the audience would often mistakenly think he was being humorous and would greet his efforts with hoots of laughter. The president was determined that the Dewan should not speak at the college; but the concluding announcement of the generous gift of a hundred thousand rupees completely altered the situation, and the president forgot the Dewan's defects. Now all he wanted was to get the details arranged at once so that delay should not intervene and give the Dewan time to reconsider his offer. He folded his hands respectfully and, with a cringing smile spreading across his face, he said, almost as if he were reciting a petition to a Maharajah: "Dewan Sahib, you and your illustrious family have done more to advance the cause of learning in our city than anyone else. We accept your gracious gift, and we will immediately name the department after you. I will go at once to the leading portrait-painter and ask him to donate to the college a portrait of your honourable self. Please decide whether you will wish to decorate the walls of our Hall in the traditional dress of your family or in academic robes."

Ram Nath took all this for granted. But his main point was being lost sight of, and that must not be. Again he moved forward in his chair and waved his arm impatiently. "Yes, yes. But what about the announcement. Are we not to have the meeting at the college?"

The president gaped, but, remembering the gift, he recovered himself and said rapidly: "Yes, your honour. We must of course have a meeting. You will speak and the people will listen to your words of wisdom. We will arrange it all. It will be the most important meeting we have ever had."

It was all arranged and, bowing very low, the dignitaries from the college withdrew.

When they left, the Dewan sighed. He was a sensitive person and their cringing response to his offer had been loathsome to him. Was there an unbridgeable gulf between the good—as represented by himself in this case—and the people to whom one tried to extend the good—represented by these cringing college folk? He was conscious of a great distance between himself and the ordinary mortals around him.

Feeling full of virtue and exaltation, he went into his private study to look at some interesting commentaries on the Upanishads which a friend had just sent him. He sank into a deep leather chair and opened the first volume. But he could not concentrate. He found that he was still thinking of his own virtues. Only, now the thought was like a great weight upon him. He was troubled by his own capacity for goodness. It was not that he considered himself to have acted rashly or over-generously. He had plenty of money and would not miss what he was giving away. No, it was not that; but he was definitely unnerved by what he had done. He shrank even from the memory of his good deed.

Something in him cried out for the obliteration of this thing. And then a calm but cunning thought enticed him. Raja Muzaffar Khan was the man he should see. Muzaffar would take him out to that delightful place in the country. There was another woman there now; yes, the Raja had told him that. And this time he would not have to sit against the pillow, nibbling nuts and listening to Muzaffar disporting himself behind a screen. The thought was delightful and overpowering. He got up and rushed to the telephone. He called the Raja Sahib, but Muzaffar was out and it was not known when he would return.

What was he to do now? Ram Nath tried to comfort himself, but a deeply inbred pride quickly rejected any self-pity. Why should he be ashamed of what he had done? After all, it was something to be proud of. The college would remember him forever, and, whatever some people might say, it was absolutely essential to study the intricacies of the art of government. Little had been done in the country in this field since the days of Chanukya and Manu, about two thousand years ago. And so, laboriously, Ram Nath tried to justify to himself the deed to which he had committed himself. He felt a little more at ease and decided to take a stroll in the garden. On the main lawn, his brother's grandchildren and some of their friends were playing cricket. It pleased him to see them at play, but they were so close to a bed of roses that every few minutes they went racing through it after the ball. He pointed out what they were doing, and they immediately moved the stumps to another part of the sward. Their response pleased him and he resumed his walk.

In another part of the garden he came upon a gardener
weeding a flower bed. He lingered to look at the man at
work and showed him that there were still some weeds in
the part of the bed which he was supposed to have cleared.
The gardener bowed low to the Dewan and at once started
again at the beginning of the bed, this time working very
thoroughly.

The Dewan went on with his walk, but the oppression of
his good deeds was heavier than ever. Why was it, he asked
himself, that even when he sought to relax in his own garden, he had to correct one thing or another? It took away
the joy of being in the garden. He went back to his room.
The telephone rang. It was Muzaffar returning his call.

Strangely enough, Ram Nath found himself telling the
Raja just the thing from which he thought he wanted to
escape.

Everything was grist to the mill of Muzaffar's hedonistic
monism, even gifts for the study of the art of government.
With true innocence and in a hearty voice, he said: "Wonderful, my dear Ram Nath, wonderful! You are a great man.
God will bless you. You are always doing things for other
people. But now you must allow life to reward you. We will
celebrate this event. Let us enjoy ourselves at Adampur. I
really oughtn't to invite you since you spurned my invitation
last time, but, come, let us go."

Ram Nath was again gripped by his earlier compulsion to
go to Adampur and he had no intention of missing this opportunity—but his reply to the Raja had to be in keeping
with the pattern of life he tried to display to the world.

"Raja Sahib, thank you for your invitation. As a matter of
fact, I was going to be busy tonight doing other things, but

I will cancel my other plans and spend the evening with you. We will go wherever you please."

The two friends did go to Adampur, and things went more or less as Ram Nath had hoped. Ranu had a friend on hand and it was decided that she would be the Dewan's companion for the evening—but Muzaffar was so taken with her that he was unable to resist keeping her for himself, so that Ram Nath had to take Ranu. It was a bit upsetting to the Dewan to be with a woman whom he knew to be very intimate with the Raja. But soon Ram Nath forgot about this. The only really annoying feature was that there was but one screen. The Raja went behind it, while Ram Nath and his new friend had to remain on the open terrace. Of course, it was in the dark of night, but it was quite likely that some of the servants were peeping at them from the door of the house.

When Ram Nath returned home next morning at about five, he was tired but elated. He felt much more at peace with himself. He even seemed to understand more fully why it was good to endow chairs at colleges to promote the study of the liberal arts. Life again had meaning; it had a fullness and richness of which he was only just becoming aware. He even felt that he was part of that richness, and not just a vehicle of the principle of good.

CHAPTER TWELVE

THE NEXT DAY, when Jai's eyes opened and he was conscious again of the morning, he felt that he had awakened in entirely strange surroundings. He remembered his early childhood visits with the family to the Chamba Hills in the Himalayas, where each time the first morning had a different scent and the new air flowing in his lungs made them feel like many-branched trees awakening. The sounds, the colours, the texture of people's voices and even the meaning of their words, old familiar words, seemed different. Today again, in his humdrum apartment at Delhi, there was all this intense sensation of discovery. He remembered Lena and her visit of the previous day, and that was like the finding of the clue; with this discovery, the feeling of strangeness became assimilated and central, and, if anything, more intense and invigorating than at his first consciousness of it. Stiff in his plaster, he got out of bed, still somewhat painfully, and his bare feet felt the delight of the cool stone tiles.

There was a knock at the door. Jai opened it. A meek-looking man with a straggling moustache, dressed in a khaki Government uniform, stood before him. The surprise of seeing a representative of the Government sent little reflexes of sharp pain through all Jai's bruises. What could this be? But it was only a messenger from the telegraph office. Jai took the flimsy buff envelope and shut the door. He opened the envelope. As he read, it was as though he had gone into the wrong door; as though the man in khaki had come to the wrong door. So he read it again. It was now clear to him. His mother was dead. "Come at once," said the telegram.

Jai felt himself clambering from the peak of love to the peak of death. All the tenderness of his mother swept through him. He stood drenched with this feeling. Then he stirred himself into action. He would have to go on his journey without getting in touch with his friends or with Lena, for they would insist that he was not well enough to travel.

He left a note for Shabir, painfully packed a valise, and took a tonga to the citadel-like railway station. Entering it, he felt that he was being swallowed up by his past life.

Late in the evening he arrived at Gurdaspur, and from there he jogged uncomfortably for an hour and a half in an old tonga that took him to their village home twelve miles away at Harbanspura. Though he was in pain, the train journey had calmed him.

When he arrived home he found that, as he had expected, his mother's body had already been cremated and the ashes collected in a little urn to be taken to Hardwar, where the sacred river Ganga emerged from the Himalayas to flow into the needy plains of India.

Jai's father was sitting in the courtyard of the family home with about twenty men—relatives and friends—all of them

silent. From a room in the house came the wailing sound of
the women weeping. Jai sat down and looked at his father's
face. It was a gentle, thoughtful physiognomy. Jai couldn't
tell whether it showed grief or not. In a sense, of course, it
reflected his sorrow, but it was no different at all from the
face he had always known. It was as though Prem Singh had
always lived with death, with this death; or perhaps he was
still living the life that he had had with his wife. So it
seemed, at any rate to Jai, that the two summits of love and
death had become one in his father's life. That comforted
Jai, but somehow he was afraid. If he became like that,
would the others—would Lena—understand it? And could
he really be like that? Could he combine his past, his family,
the sense of mother-love that filled him, with his absorption
in the movement for freedom and with the new strangeness
of love?

Jai stayed very quietly in his room for three days. He saw
no one and was, of course, not expected to. Much of the time
he was in a sort of coma of convalescence, and put up no
fight against it. Came the ceremonies fixed for the fourth
day. The Brahmins read verses from the scriptures till nones,
and in the mid-afternoon almost all the menfolk of the village gathered in the courtyard of Prem Singh's house. The
women gathered in the room to the west of the courtyard
and overflowed on the outer side. This was the last homage
of the community in which Jai's mother had lived.

That evening Jai took the train back to Delhi. The journey
back to the struggle for freedom and to the tenderness of love
that Jai thought he was entering was like a beginning. It
was, to Jai, as though his mother somehow had elected this
time to die so as to simplify his life for him; as though she
felt that by withdrawing and leaving him the memory of

her love, she could still sustain him and yet free him for
those new peaks that he had to climb. She had died in order
to give him more space to himself. Was it like that—this laying down of life by one generation so that the next might
reach out to life? It seemed so. It was cruel in a way but also
immensely tender, and it was the latter feeling that seemed
to become imbedded in Jai as the train brought him back to
Delhi.

For Lena, these days of Jai's absence brought another kind
of crescendo. She was bewildered by Jai's having left without
getting in touch with her. She knew he was not in Delhi because he was not at the meetings of their group of workers,
and then Shabir told her at one of the meetings that he had
gone to his village. She felt stranded. And, not hearing from
Jai, she began to wonder whether she had not done something that was really outside her place in the scheme of
things. Certainly none of her relatives nor her mother would
have allowed herself this sort of romanticism.

Two days after Jai had left Delhi, the whole Dharma Das
household was awakened at two in the morning. Lena heard
the authoritarian sound of heavy boots on the front veranda
and of people talking as if they were walking through a
public park where often people felt they must speak loud
enough to fill the vast open space around them. Then she
heard the maid Gangi's footsteps and the thud of her anklets,
all much quicker than usual. Then came Gangi's call, in a
quavering, almost wailing voice, to Shanti Devi:

"Bibiji, Bibiji, it's the police! Ram! Ram! Sita Ram! What
have we done!"

Curiously, that relieved Lena's tension. The police! It was
like the name of a familiar phenomenon that had become the

inevitable undertone of life. Only the police, that was all.

Lena quickly put on a sari, and as she entered the corridor so, too, did her mother also now in a sari, and her father, Dharma Das, with a heavy Kashmiri shawl thrown over his pyjamas. Shanti Devi opened the front door.

Before them stood a handsome Indian police officer with scimitar-like moustaches. He clicked his heels and saluted smartly. Again Lena felt at ease. All this was somehow part of the daily situation and she felt a clever sureness within herself: they would somehow get round whatever the police had planned on this occasion.

The police officer said politely but crisply that he had brought a warrant for the arrest of Shanti Devi. Lena felt the blood drain away from her face. She hoped no one had noticed this annoying reflex. But already she was recovering some of her poise on hearing her father, who now seemed to be saving the situation. In his most friendly manner, one that Lena had seldom heard him use, he said:

"Yes, yes, Sub-Inspector Sahib, but under what section of the law do you come to apprehend my wife?"

The police officer said with a sort of quick, intelligent ignorance: "I do not know, Panditji."

"Then your warrant is illegal, Sahib," replied Dharma Das, adopting the tone he used in court when he had established a point.

The sub-inspector stood very straight, as though Ram Das's well-earned point was a personal insult. Lena again felt that all was lost. The man might do anything now, and her eyes seemed charmed by the heavy black holster on his belt and the thick black butt of his service revolver. But the police officer decided to keep to civil speech, in which form of expression he had but limited competence, so he repeated, but more crisply this time:

"I do not know, Sir!"

Dharma Das thought it best not to probe further. The police officer said that Shanti Devi could have half an hour to collect a few changes of clothes. Once again during this period Dharma Das asked a question. This time he meekly enquired where Shanti Devi would be taken. The sub-inspector glared at him for a few seconds and then again shot out the words: "I do not know."

Before this, Lena realized that they had lost. At the point of that realization, the abject fear into which she had sunk seemed to lift. Something hardened in her and rose right through her body in a cold fury. Now she faced the police officer and, her dark eyes flashing, she challenged his action.

"How dare you arrest my mother and not me when I, too, was at the river! Don't you know that it was I who took the water from the river and lit the fire in the brazier? I am the really guilty one. You must arrest me!"

But the police officer, whose manliness was deeply stirred by this beautiful, spirited girl, twirled his scimitar-like moustaches and smiled. He clicked his heels gallantly and said, as if with some regret: "I have no warrant for Lena Devi."

Lena wept bitterly when the police car drove away with her mother. She wept not out of weakness but out of the frustration she felt in the face of the silly arbitrariness of the police. The weeping, which she could not control, made her feel very helpless and weak and yet it seemed to leave within her a tremendous strength. Did they think that, being young, she would be unable to defy their unjust laws? In her tears and confusion, she vowed she would show them that they were mistaken. The whole experience created in her a hardness, and she ceased to wonder about Jai's absence.

CHAPTER THIRTEEN

WHEN Ram Nath thought, as he often did, of the onward flow of life, of the generation that would succeed to the world when he left it, these thoughts were apotheosized for him in Geeta, his beautiful young niece. Somehow he couldn't think of his son, Dina Nath, as the inheritor of the world—his world. But Geeta seemed to him already to be setting out in a blaze of glory, and the vision of her future life imparted glowing warmth to his advancing age.

As Brij Krishen, her father, was in the thick of the national struggle—her mother long since being dead—Geeta had come to Delhi again to spend some time at Dewan House. The visit suited her well. She thought one of Ram Nath's young secretaries exceedingly handsome and she had already made that known to him during her last visit. He was, in truth, a rather weak person who daydreamed about success, good food, fine clothes, and the swooning passions of women brought to his arms. The dream world in which he lived gave his light brown-green eyes a rather exciting look; so, at any rate, thought Geeta. She had smiled at him several times, and on one occasion when she was handing him some letters to post, she had held his hand with some passion.

Geeta had returned to Dewan House impatient to fulfil her promise to herself regarding Amir Chand, the young secretary. To her delight, he was the first person she met as she entered the house. She smiled warmly at him, and he greeted her with his daydreaming eyes looking unboundedly romantic. Later that day, when Ram Nath had gone out, she went into his office and asked Amir Chand to come round to the outer door of her bedroom at about seven in the evening —as soon as it was dark. Seeing the perplexed look with which Amir Chand responded, she quickly added that she expected to have some letters ready for the mail.

That evening Geeta lay on her bed in a fever of excitement. Each second her body traversed a universe, seeking the hour when Amir Chand would visit her. As the light outside faded, her body seemed to run faster and faster till she was in a bath of sweat and her hands and feet twitched nervously.

At last Amir Chand came. Geeta practically hurled herself at him. It was all much fiercer than the graceful, mellow daydreams that filled his mind. Amir Chand felt like running away, but it would have been easier to escape from a hungry tigress. Soon Geeta became calmer, exhausted by her own efforts. The change seemed to kindle Amir Chand, and Geeta finally got more or less what she had wanted.

But when Amir Chand left—after about an hour—her

feeling was one of relief. To her, he had been half-witted and insipid. Now her fury rose again, and this time it turned on herself. Why had she given herself to such piffling canaille! She wanted to tear the whole thing out of her life. She laughed to herself. She would get Amir Chand out of the house. He would not be around to remind her of her folly.

The next day she said to him sharply, within the hearing of Ram Nath: "Now, post these letters at once. My friends are not used to any delay in hearing from me!" Amir Chand looked at her in utter confusion as, silently, he took the letters. She had rightly adjudged him far too much of a weakling to stand up for himself.

Ram Nath heard Geeta's sharp words to Amir Chand. He himself regarded Amir Chand more as a pensionnaire than as a worker. The man never could trace any papers that Ram Nath wanted, but, so far, the Dewan had for some reason found no difficulty in tolerating Amir Chand's general slackness. But when he heard Geeta, he came rapidly to her side, his face white with anger, and to her words he added: "Get on to your bicycle and post those letters at once, do you hear, you goose-faced minion!"

Amir Chand turned slowly away, wondering what had happened. Geeta felt herself completely in the right when Ram Nath had delivered himself of his broadside. Now was the time to press on with her attack. Taking Ram Nath's arm, she said in a tart combination of sweetness and contempt: "My dearest Uncle, that man is an idiot! Don't know how you could ever have engaged him."

Amir Chand set out for the post office—he dared not consign these fateful letters to a letter-box. He got to the post office and carefully locked his bicycle in the stand. He went to the mail-box with the reverence with which one might approach a god or an altar. He put his hand into his pocket to extract his offering. There were no letters. He tried all the other pockets. He shook his jacket. No, the letters were not there. He looked at the flat red face of the mail-box—he felt that the god had rejected him.

In deep gloom, Amir Chand cycled back to Dewan House, a mile and a half away. His daydreams gave place to a nightmare of fear. When he arrived at the office, there was the Dewan waiting for him.

"Have you posted the letters?" he asked sternly. Amir Chand dared not face his master. His eyes scanned his desk. The letters lay in front of him. Ram Nath saw him grab at them and he thought Amir Chand had gone mad. And, indeed, Amir Chand felt that he was out of his mind. Grasping the letters, he turned and ran to his bicycle. Swinging on to it, he set out again.

It was all so insane that Ram Nath's rage subsided. "Poor idiot!" he sighed. "The man is a natural-born fool. I will send him out to my Bareilly estate. There are not even bicycles there, and no urgent orders!"

Then Ram Nath remembered that Geeta had just told him that the man was an idiot. How unerringly right that beautiful girl was! Yes, she was his idea of how life should go on. How quickly, without knowing Amir Chand—how could she know him?—she had sized him up. Yes, she was wonderful! Ram Nath smiled to himself and decided that he must express his delight in Geeta.

He went to the small safe in his bedroom and took from it a beautiful string of large, uncut emeralds on a gold chain. It was an heirloom that he had never brought himself to give to his wife. Somehow it was too vivid for the quiet-natured Rajeshwari. The emerald string had a curious history. It was said to have been given by a ruler of the Punjab to his mistress about a century before. How it had found its way into the Dewan's family, Ram Nath had never cared to ascertain, as he felt certain he would be easier in his mind if not too enlightened about the matter. He held it up and its glow confirmed him in his decision. The necklace seemed to him perfect for Geeta, and he erased from his mind the history of the jewels, for it was, of course, inappropriate to the new phase it was about to enter with his innocent niece.

Ram Nath put the jewels in his pocket and went in search of Geeta. On the front veranda was a handsome young man dressed in simple hand-woven white material. Ram Nath went up to him, wondering who it might be. Jai turned to him. The Dewan immediately recognized him. He had liked Jai Singh from the very first time they had met. He put his hand heartily on Jai's shoulder and said: "Welcome to you, Jai Singh. It's a pleasure to see you here." Then he thought a moment. Well, why shouldn't this fine-looking young man see how he treated his niece? Just then Geeta came on to the veranda. That settled it—Jai Singh would witness the presentation.

Geeta was smouldering and sulky. She came out of her room aimlessly, not knowing what to do with herself. She had come to Delhi ostensibly to be with the Dewan and his family because her father was busy with national affairs, but she could just as well have stayed at home in Lucknow. What had really brought her was her interest in Amir Chand. Now that that had so easily rubbed off, she wanted something new to absorb her.

Ram Nath called to her brightly, not noticing her sulks—which, however, did not escape Jai's attention.

"Come, my darling child," said Ram Nath, raising an arm

toward her. "I was just going in search of you because—because— Well, you shall see why." Then Ram Nath turned to Jai Singh. "Lovely, lovely, isn't she? God is very good to us, really!"

Jai Singh said nothing to Ram Nath, but looked again at the sulky young woman walking languidly toward them. In response to what the Dewan had just said, she was grimacing a smile. Jai had no desire for another meeting with Geeta, but there was a kind of suppressed glow on her face which, in spite of himself, he wanted to release and to know about.

Geeta had now come up to them. With a quick movement, Ram Nath took the string from his pocket and held it before her. It was very striking, and Geeta's eyes fastened on it. Ram Nath was delighted that the stones had caught her attention, and kept glancing from her face to the string in a crescendo of admiration. To Jai, Geeta's bright eyes seemed harder even than the stones, but still her face glowed, and the combination tantalized him.

"Yes, yes. It is handsome," said Ram Nath, nodding his head slowly as if to keep time with the slowly moving stones. Then he added, with a warm smile, putting his arm through Geeta's: "And, my dear, dear child, it is for you!" He turned and looked at her.

Geeta's eyes were very bright now. She did genuinely love her uncle and this demonstration of his affection moved her. The glow on her face softened as she took the stones from Ram Nath, who was thrusting them into her hand. She closed her fist on them and said to him: "How kind, how good you are, Uncle. I don't deserve all this from you!"

Ram Nath put his arm around her. "Don't deserve this!" And he turned her toward Jai Singh as if showing her off to him. "Look at her," he said. "She is what we should try to make of the young people of India, and yet she says she doesn't deserve this little bauble I have given her!"

Jai Singh did not know what to say. Perhaps the Dewan was right. He could feel the strength of Geeta's personality, but he could not say what she was like. To him she was beautiful, yes, but self-indulgent, arrogant—and there was more than a hint of a certain ruthlessness about the way she thrust out her chin.

Geeta, too, was looking at Jai. Yes, he was handsome—but remote; didn't know himself as a man, she thought. But he was very attractive to her. And she felt that this was no piffling nobody. He was strong, real, and intense in his own way. She kept looking at him.

The Dewan smiled at Geeta again and released her from his arm. With Jai Singh, he went off to his study.

CHAPTER FOURTEEN

JAI HAD BEEN in Delhi two days when he met Lena outside Mool Chand's, a fashionable store near Kashmiri Gate which sold all kinds of imported goods. The store was being picketed as part of the program of discouraging the purchase and use of British goods. There was a tense, unruly situation outside the store. Every five minutes the police arrested the picket lines, to an accompaniment of derisive shouting from the thousands of citizens who had gathered at the scene; and then, immediately following, would come the thundering cheer "Victory to Gandhiji!" as a fresh group of pickets took the place of those arrested. Often, persons from the crowd who happened to have stopped to watch and who were expecting to be at home in a half-hour or so would have the normal course of their lives drastically interrupted by joining the pickets and being whisked off to the police lockup and then to prison for a year or so.

Lena and Jai were not courting arrest on this occasion, but

both were present in order to be with the other workers and their friends.

Jai went up to Lena, full of his love for her. He was conscious of the glow and smile on his face. He struggled to bring down his expression a peg or two when he noticed the drawn look on her face. He knew that her mother had been arrested and jailed, but he did not know of Lena's deep, unswerving vow. She looked at him and smiled, her eyes meeting his, and then quickly her glance withdrew and seemed to excuse itself. Jai's eyes appealed to her for some explanation. She seemed to flounder for the right idiom of response, torn by her love for him and the demands of her new acolytic stage. For an eternal second Jai stood by, helplessly watching, but her answer never came. A young girl volunteer ran up to Lena and said that her advice was wanted by the workers. Without even turning to Jai, Lena turned away.

Just then a derisive shout from the crowd as the police arrested another row of pickets intruded on the intensity of Jai's anguish. He felt unprotected, alien almost, among these people with whom he worked and lived. He looked at the stretch of grass alongside the pavement just outside Kashmiri Gate, and his feet had started to move in that direction when he heard a call.

"Young leader! Young leader!"

Automatically he turned. A group of men, including Shabir, were beckoning to him frantically. He stopped, nothing in him really responding. The beckoning grew more desperate. Shabir called now:

"Jai, come here, quickly!"

A shrill whistle sounded. A police officer howled out an order that made no sense to Jai's ears. Scores of police standing near their vans rushed in among the crowd and hit out

with their batons and staves. The passers-by, who had been
enjoying the spectacle and joining in the shouting, ran for
their lives. The police seemed to think that they had achieved
their objective. They contented themselves with arresting the
picket line and a few volunteers standing near it. Lena left
with some of the injured women. Jai, still feeling very de-
tached, walked away with Shabir.

In the early hours of a May morning came the news that
in the dead of the previous night a police party, heavily
armed, had entered the hut in which Gandhi was staying
near Bombay and had arrested him. The British had for
weeks been baffled and in despair at the continuing strength
of the Movement. They argued that if Gandhi were put in
heavily guarded segregation, the nerve center of the Movement would be cut off from the people.

The less scrupulous members of the Administration saw a
more sharply decisive argument for the arrest of Gandhi.
They hoped that the deed would provoke the people to violence. Then the rulers would be justified in using the stern-
est measures to repress the Movement: the leaders in each
locality could be shot, and that would effectively destroy the
Movement for a generation. So, for various reasons, all the
people on the Government side hailed the arrest as a wonderful piece of strategy.

The news would soon seethe through the crowds of Delhi
and the people would be impatient to express their resentment, despair, anguish, and anger. There was no time to be
lost. On hearing the news, Jai went immediately to the place
designated as the headquarters of the Movement for that
day. It was Pandit Dharma Das's house. Jai found Lena
alone in the western veranda. She was looking at the seven-
o'clock morning scene: the dew still gleamed on the close-cut

grass of the lawn, and a brown-and-gold songbird was calling with a throaty sweetness, while the minas twittered greedily as they picked at the turf. Beyond the lawn, the shy lavender bloom of the slender Persian lilacs gave the edge of the morning sky a firmness of blue which would soon, as the sun advanced, burnish into the hard glint of steel grey.

Jai, too, waited a moment and looked at the beauty of the morning. Then he turned to the lovely girl on the veranda, communicating so serenely with nature. Her face was pale, but seemed in deep repose, as though this moment of political crisis had become thoroughly integrated, leaving in her no insoluble questions or anxieties.

Jai did not put his feelings for Lena into words—not even to himself—but he had come there today very much aware of how deep they were. Seeing her now in contemplation, he greeted her quietly. She looked up, and when she saw him, her pale face was immediately all radiant and her eyes sought him out in his innermost being. His whole body was clamorous again. He went up to her and held out his hand. She took it readily. Then she shook her head slowly and said to him with the depth of her eyes and also with her lips: "Yes, Jai, but not just now. Wait."

They unlinked hands and Jai sat down beside her. He, too, wanted to talk about the things that urgently had to be arranged. All the older leaders in Delhi had already been arrested, and now it was for these young people and the other younger leaders, who would soon be arriving, to decide on the activities of the next few days.

Lena was the first to speak. Very quietly and in an even voice, she said to him: "Jai, our test has come at last. Now we will find out whether this thing that Gandhiji has been trying to implant in us has taken root."

Jai somehow expected her to be calm and determined, but he wondered whether she had thought the matter through. "Yes, this is the test. But how do you think we can meet it?" he asked.

Without hesitation she replied: "I do not know the complete answer, but I am certain that today I must lead the protest procession."

Jai was alarmed at this decision. "But how can you come to such a decision! You know, we must think this out very carefully. Today will be especially dangerous. The police are sure to be reinforced by units of troops from the Fort. It might even shake the Government more effectively if we were not to have a procession today."

She shook her head. "Someone must stand up to any danger that comes. You see, the reason I feel I should lead the procession is that, whatever happens, today our people must remain specially disciplined. I am sure it is part of the test that today, of all days, we must be completely non-violent. If I lead the procession—I, a woman—they will realize that they must be their gentlest."

"But if you are arrested, or wounded, it might have the opposite effect, Lena."

But she would not listen. She was convinced that if she led the procession, it would help the people keep to what Gandhi had taught them. When the other leaders arrived, she announced her decision. Again there were protests. But when she explained her reason, they were silent.

As the young leaders were leaving for the public park outside the Kashmiri Gate of the city, news came that the authorities had proclaimed that if more than four people met together in a public place, they would be immediately dispersed by the use of effective measures, including force. This was precisely as Jai and some of the others had feared. For a moment they stopped and looked at one another in silence, but the next moment brought the unanimous and spontaneous reiteration of their decision to hold a meeting of protest against the arrest of the leader of the country.

The whole populace of the city was roused to a fury of resentment that, unprovoked, the uniformed minions of an irresponsible law should have dared in the dead of night to invade the privacy and quiet of their leader. At this moment the cleavage between the people and the foreign ruler seemed absolute, and Jai feared, especially when he thought of the role that Lena had decided to play, that some terrible clash was imminent.

The people heard the order against public meetings, but still they came out of their homes by the thousand, seeing in the proclamation only another instance of the arbitrariness of the Government. They had heard that the leaders were headed for the public park. It was then that the most extraordinary event in the long history of Delhi occurred, an event that even Mohammed Shah Tughlak, the fourteenth-century autocrat, had failed to bring about when he ordered the people, under pain of the severest punishment, to evacuate the old city and settle at his new capital, Tughlakabad, ten miles from Delhi. To meet with the leaders in the park, the whole city now became a moving stream. Through the streets of Delhi, every living thing moved in the direction of the park. Hackney carriages, cars, tongas, and bicycles, which had set out on their usual daily tasks in various parts of the city, found the press of the current of this human stream so great that all of them had to flow with it. So, too, did the stray dogs, the beggars—many of whom normally pretended to be paralysed—cows and camels, and even the postmen and hawkers who happened to be on their morning rounds. All shops and places of business closed as a protest against the arrest of Gandhi, and indeed there was no one now to tend them.

The authorities were not prepared for this moving metropolitan river. Most of the leaders and their supporters were in jail, and so many of the enthusiastic workers had been killed, injured, or jailed that it had been calculated that the most that could happen would be an ill-attended protest meeting. The administrators looked on, exasperated and helpless, at the dense waves of people moving through the streets of Delhi and chanting the name of Gandhi and calling "Hey Ram, Hey Ram" or "Allah—o—Akbar." Their orderliness and their calling on God infuriated the self-righteous authorities.

The head of the Administration, his face red and his veins bulging, looked angrily at the head of the police and the other senior officers and shouted at them: "Why the hell was I not informed at any time that there were so many people in Delhi!" Of course, there had been a census, but no one dared point that out.

Then he shouted again: "And where are all those damned bastards—thousands of them—who came cringing to take our honours and ribbons—the Rai Sahibs, Khan Bahadurs, Knights, and the other toadies!" No one answered.

Yes, where were all those thousands of people who had subscribed to the Viceroy's Fund and had been to parties at the Viceroy's palace? Could they not be mustered now in a counter-demonstration? But, curiously, the officers could not think of the names of more than a handful of "loyal" citizens. There was Sir Ramji Das, but he was holidaying up at one of the gayest of the hill resorts. He could normally be counted on to collect a small group of persons to be present at a pro-Government meeting.

Everyone in the official camp was in despair till a young police office volunteered to get the force to the park by driving along a little-used route to the river and then bringing the men in again from the north, where there was little habitation and therefore only a thin trickle of people would be coming in for the meeting. The senior officers of the Administration were too confused to be able to decide whether they should accept this suggestion. The young officer saluted smartly and repeated his request for orders. The silence remained unbroken. The officer decided to act on his own. He clicked his heels and saluted again. Then, jumping into a police car with a few other junior officers, he rushed off to execute his plan.

Meanwhile, the leaders and tens of thousands of people had reached the park, and the meeting was in session. Lena was telling the people that they must now be prepared for greater severity from the Government, and that their only response could be to give up all connection with the foreign ruler—but to do so not only without any violence but also without any bitterness. To many of the people, incensed at the arrest of their saintly leader and hoping for orders to march on Delhi to take over the government, this was utterly unacceptable at first. But when Lena—young, collected, and full of faith in the success of the Movement—passionately implored them to stick unswervingly to Gandhi's rule of non-violence, they were ashamed of their feelings. Their desire for revenge turned into a determination to follow their arrested leader's teachings. The crowd had swelled to several hundred thousand. It responded with cries of "Victory to Gandhi!" when Lena suggested that they should all walk in orderly procession to the office of the head of the Administration and remain standing in front of the Administration Building throughout that day to register their protest.

Lena and the others who had been conducting the meeting stepped off the old brick platform that had been built many years before for performances in the park by the Viceroy's band. The crowd made way for them and then surged behind. It was at this point that the armed police, led by the daring young officer, completed their circuitous course to the park and bore down on the vast crowd.

The young officer, flushed with a sense of high valour and heroism, gave his men orders to charge the crowd—he thought it an act of vital importance for the survival of the British Empire and for the glory of Imperial traditions. The relatively small force of armed men—perhaps one hundred and fifty in all—could easily have been surrounded and disarmed by the crowd. But the rule of Gandhi was that no force at all was to be used by those who accepted participation in the Movement—it was the only way, said Gandhi, that those who used force could learn the futility and inhumanity of their weapons.

The police, led by young officers full of the excitement and callousness of youth, hit out hard with their heavy steel-headed staves and their rifle butts. Many hundreds in the crowd were injured and many ran to save themselves. The police column was now approaching the group of leaders. The men formed thick ranks around Lena. But the police officers were bent on getting to the leaders and taking them off as proof to their superiors of a job well done. So the men who were around Lena, and the group with her—which included Jai and Shabir—were struck down.

Others rushed to take their place. Among them was Munshi Ram, the rich young landlord who had originally joined the Movement just to be in the good books of a powerful body of public opinion. But, now, much deeper impulsions were at work. He bounded forward to protect Lena. Immediately a heavy police staff hit him. He fell, but quickly struggled to his feet and, not being fully aware of the rules of the game, he clung to the policeman's staff to prevent its being aimed at Lena. Being very heavily built and ungainly, his pulling at the staff unbalanced both himself and the constable, and the two of them fell. In the melee, it looked as though the constable might be trampled underfoot. One of the young British officers saw the situation. It was more than he could stand, and, fired by his loyalty to one of his men, he whipped out his pistol and shot Munshi Ram.

Hearing the shot, the police concluded that a general order to open fire had been given. Sighting their rifles on the crowd, they released about two hundred rounds of ammunition. The people fled in all directions, and the park was in utter disorder. The dust rose thick, and there was the wailing of the wounded, and the shouting of their companions, and the calls for help and mercy.

Panic also seized the police. The young officers, who till a moment ago had regarded themselves as brave and heroic, were unnerved. They feared that something terrible was about to happen. Perhaps the crowd, which looked as if it was fleeing, was really going off in the direction of the British residential area and would massacre men, women, and children. There were no police in that section to defend it. Forgetting their previous objective of carrying off the leaders, the police offcers called in their men, rushed to their trucks, and made off to protect their kith and kin from the supposed but utterly fatuous danger.

Jai had been injured again. Lena, too, had been hit on the right shoulder and was in great pain. Still, she went up to the prostrate Munshi Ram, who lay groaning in the dust and dirt. He had lost a great deal of blood, but was still breathing. Lena tried to tear off a piece of her sari, but was unable to manage it with her uninjured arm. Jai crawled to her, and together they succeeded. They bandaged Munshi Ram's chest, and by the time this was done, he had stopped groaning. He lay there silently, looking very bloated and ungainly. A little gore was congealing at the side of his mouth. Lena and Jai looked helplessly at him. There was nothing they could do. Lena took his head in her lap and Jai tried to massage his hands and feet. The body grew cold. Munshi Ram was dead.

Lena and Jai helped each other up. The police had disappeared. Only a few hundred people remained, tending the injured and removing them. Jai had to lean on Lena, but she, too, was weak and could barely walk. As they wobbled along together, Lena smiled faintly as if something hopeful had occurred to her. Jai looked at her questioningly. Very quietly she said:

"It is all very sad—this brutality and destruction. And yet the counteracting thing is so amazing. I never expected people like Munshi Ram to give their lives."

With great difficulty, the two struggled on till they reached Lena's house. Pandit Dharma Das, her father, was one of the very few in the city who had not gone to the park. The whole morning he had been terribly tense and his face had turned grey. Then he had heard the sound of the firing and had feared the worst. He had known that his daughter would be in the thick of things. When he saw her come up the driveway in a most unusual manner—Lena and Jai were still leaning on each other—he ran to her. With the help of the servants, the wounded young people were brought into the house.

When the police trucks reached the other side of the city, they drew up and waited for the onrush of the people. But the people had no idea such as that with which the police had credited them: they simply went home, and none of them committed any violence. The young police officers could not believe this. They were sure that some sinister plan was afoot and that a great attack would any moment be unleashed against the British. It never occurred to them that they were dealing, not with a band of dacoits or with a specific foe, but with a whole people who had decided to go forward into their own future, and who rejected the view that the only way of doing this was by applying violence to the obstacles in their path.

The hours passed, and no attack came. The young officers realized that they had made a mistake. How could they now return to their superior officers without being able to tell them that they had taken into custody the ringleaders of the Movement? Hastily they took counsel among themselves and decided that they must set out again with a couple of truckloads of armed men—they still were too afraid to move around in the city, among these people who had refused to lift a hand against them, without being heavily armed themselves. They went to the houses of the leaders whom they had seen in the park before the firing broke out. When they got to the house of Dharma Das, he begged them to leave Lena and Jai for a day or two so that they could get some rest and medical attention. But the police had their own code of behaviour to live up to, and the two young leaders were pushed into a truck and driven away.

Dharma Das was left alone. He felt his legs tremble. How, after all these years of family life, could he live alone in his large house? The soft furnishings, the paintings, and the ornate woodwork, of which he had been very proud, now were alien and comfortless. He realized how much he loved his tiresome wife, Shanti Devi, and his difficult daughter, Lena. He felt stricken right through his being. Then his body and his face suddenly grew cold and moist—he was smitten with a great fear: what if the police were to arrest him for complicity? Poor Dharma Das! Although he knew the law in all its intricacies and knew also that many times he had saved murderers from the gallows and cheats from years of imprisonment, he was now unable to find any shelter from his gripping fears. He wanted to run away. Then a fierce sense of injustice seemed to rise up in him and somewhat altered his mood. Why, why was all this happening to him? There was his friend, Dewan Ram Nath, prosperous and apparently happy, and yet he did nothing to deserve his good fortune. In fact, Ram Nath's riches were built on the chicanery, obsequiousness, and cruelty of his ancestors. Dharma Das sighed very deeply.

CHAPTER FIFTEEN

THE NEXT DAY Pandit Dharma Das visited the house of the Dewan. He did not particularly like Ram Nath, but he hoped to get some sympathy and to feel again, through the well-being of others, what life was meant to be. The Dewan was moved by the plight of the sensationally successful and prosperous lawyer, known for his monumental knowledge and his lucid, razor-like mind, whose face now looked confused and almost babyish, and whose large figure had slumped into an ungainly mass without any dignity.

"Come, Dharma Das," he said with genuine sympathy. "Stay with us for a few days—for as long as you like. My humble home is open to you. The world, my dear friend, is going quite mad. I no longer understand anything."

Dharma Das sighed heavily. His eyes filled with tears. He had always regarded the Dewan as incapable of understanding anything about people, ideas, history, or the law. But, still, the Dewan had everything that life could provide. In a breaking voice, Dharma Das said: "Everything has been taken from me. I never expected this: to be forced into a life of solitary renunciation. I now have nothing. Nothing. So that the question of understanding life doesn't even exist for me. What good trying to understand what is denied to one?"

Dewan Ram Nath looked very sad. He decided that from himself, too, almost everything had been taken away. He nodded his head and said: "Yes, Dharma Das, you are right. What meaning can life have when it has withdrawn from us? I, too, feel that life has passed me by, probably forever." And he sighed deeply while his alert little face tried to fall in line and his eyes became quite misty.

Dharma Das was perplexed and deeply hurt at this unaccountable display of self-pity by the Dewan. What was the use of coming here? He was getting little sympathy even though it must have been obvious how cruelly he had been treated by fate. He decided to get up and leave.

Just then the Dewan's wilful niece, Geeta, came into the study. Although she herself looked uninspiringly sulky and ill-tempered, Ram Nath greeted her with a complete reversal of his mood of sadness. He pulled at his little beard and, breaking into a smile, he said:

"Come in, my dear child. You are looking so beautiful, as usual—just the person to cheer us up. Poor Dharma Das," and he turned to his guest.

Geeta had read in the morning papers of Lena's arrest along with Jai. She had no intention of putting herself out and getting arrested, "and all that sort of thing," as she referred to it. Of course, she had to pay lip service to the Movement and to accept the respect accorded her as the daughter of so eminent a national leader as Pandit Brij Krishen. So now she went up to Dharma Das and, folding her hands in salutation, she said: "Yes, yes. I read it. Isn't it terrible!" She stopped a moment and then added rather angrily: "Yes, terrible." Indeed, her temper was up. She had been upset by the fact that Lena had been arrested along with Jai. It was as though she had lost something to Lena. It was this ruffled feeling that she was now expressing.

But Ram Nath understood her differently. "No, no, dear Geeta, you mustn't allow yourself to be upset by all this. I know you feel for your friend Lena, but, alas, what can we do about it?" And he sighed deeply, plunging again into his own sorrows.

Ram Nath was now thinking vaguely of the fact that he had never really had a good time, as his friend Raja Muzaffar Khan had; and he thought also of his own son's lack of distinction—he would never achieve anything worth speaking of; and, finally, there was now the distinct and frightening possibility that out of all this unrest in the country would come some sort of land-reform movement which would affect his own prosperity. He spoke as if without relevance to what had just been going on:

"I am an old man." He had never before made such an admission and the words came in a tremulous confessional voice. "Perhaps I can no longer tell good from evil. Well, that perhaps I could never do, but now I can't see any direction in human affairs. I thought the British were a sporting people. I thought they would never hit a man when he was down. But now, in front of my eyes, they arrest Gandhi when he is doing nothing. No, that is not quite right. Gandhi was only telling the people to be non-violent and to cast out all hatred of the British. Gandhi did not invent the demand for freedom. It started long ago, and it was bound to spread.

Then, couldn't the British see that Gandhi was their best friend, that he was saving them from much worse things? No, they couldn't—and they have been stupid enough to arrest him. Before this, I always said that India would have to wait a long time for her independence, but now I can't say that. The British seem just as stupid and just as blind as anyone else. Then why should we keep them here? They had better go."

The Dewan's family had been showered with many honours and had been given broad estates by the British, and Ram Nath had never said anything definitely opposed to their rule. This was something new. Pandit Dharma Das was very comforted to hear it. The Dewan's views brought solace because they made him feel that his own womenfolk were perhaps on the right side. Not that he would ever admit this to them, but it was good to know—and if they were on the right side, then they might soon be released by the Government. The argument was confused, but it comforted the old man.

To Geeta, these words were, in a way, full of sting. Again she felt jealous of Lena for taking so prominent a part in the Movement and for going to jail along with Jai. But she could not show these feelings, and it was now second nature with her to play up to her doting old uncle. Affecting a smile, she said:

"Bravo, Uncle! You are not old at all, and what you say is absolutely correct. The British are terribly incompetent, and we must take over before they mess things up any further."

Dewan Ram Nath looked at her in astonishment. For the last few weeks she had been talking against the leaders and taking no part in the Movement. Now she was saying that the country must be taken over immediately. As he looked at her, his eyes softened. She was so beautiful when aroused. He couldn't reproach her for her inconsistency, but he did have something else to say.

"Not so fast, Geeta, my dear, not so fast. We can't turn them out overnight. Indeed, I do not know whether they will ever leave. The point is simply that they have no business here any longer. We have passed through the phase when—God knows for what reason—we did need something that they could give us."

Give us? What was this? Would the British give back Shanti Devi and Lena? With these questions rushing through his mind, Dharma Das eagerly asked: "What was it they gave us?"

Ram Nath looked through the wide, low window at the garden that he loved so much. He seemed put out at the question. Then his face became unusually serious as he said: "They gave us what we very much needed—time to look at ourselves. You see, conquerors before the British never did their job thoroughly and got too much involved in the local scene. Consequently, the attrition went on continually. There never was stability under the Moghuls and, of course, still less under any of the others. The Imperial armies, in full strength, were constantly engaged in suppressing endless large-scale revolts against the authority of the foreign rulers. Indeed, such stability as the Moghuls did achieve was due not to their capacity as administrators or to their prowess as fighters—though they were, of course, very intrepid people —but to their marriages with the Rajput princesses and to their good sense in choosing many wise sons of the soil to help them establish the administration."

Pandit Dharma Das was beginning to grow uncomfortable. His distraught mind had not been able to follow the

Dewan closely, but he felt that the trend of the conversation was now somewhat in favour of the British. If this was so, his womenfolk were, after all, on the wrong side. Frightened by this terrible conclusion, he anxiously asked: "But, Ram Nath, now they must go, must they not?"

"Who can say?" answered the Dewan. "All we can say is that there is no reason now for them to stay on in the country. They have nothing more to give us. But who is going to make this clear to them? Unfortunately, they do not understand Gandhi. He tells them these things, but they regard him as a seditious agitator. And if we liberals say them, they become so incensed that it is no good at all. We think they should go. That is all I can say."

Through the open window came the cool fragrance of the eucalyptus trees. Ram Nath again looked out at the brilliantly colourful blaze of the zinnias. He was glad he had talked, and now he enjoyed the spell of silence which had fallen on the three of them. He felt that both Geeta and Dharma Das were impressed by what he had said. But Dharma Das had really hardly listened to the Dewan's words; only some few disparate phrases had linked up with his anxious, sad thoughts. And Geeta was not really interested in the Dewan's theories. Her secret annoyance at Lena continued, and she indulged now in the pleasure of observing the disconsolate Dharma Das.

But Geeta wanted to keep Ram Nath on her side. Breaking the silence, she went up to the Dewan and, taking his hand in hers, said: "Uncle, you have been wonderful today, just wonderful! We understand things much better after listening to what you have said."

Ram Nath looked up at her, his eyes warm and misty with affection and delight. He pressed her hand and sighed.

"All this is very curious. I do not feel that I really understand anything. I wish you young people would take over the affairs of life so that Dharma Das and I—and others like us—could rest."

Now it was Dharma Das who sighed. "Ram Nath, there is no laying down our burdens. Let us be truthful. For each of us the burden becomes heavier each day, and we have to go on till we can stand it no longer. Then we just give up and die." And he sighed again after this sombre announcement.

Ram Nath, in spite of his own frequent doubts about life, detested this sort of talk. "Yes, yes. That is all right, but there is a strength about old age which you must not overlook. Don't you see how young people get terribly involved in things because they have not had the experience that we have had? We conserve our capacities, but they do not because they cannot judge yet what is good for them." He ended rather abruptly, conscious that he was not so much making his point as expressing his personal dislike of Dharma Das's attitude.

Dewan Ram Nath enjoyed life far too much to agree that it was just a growing burden. What really troubled him was that he appeared to be no nearer comprehending the meaning of life than he had been as a young man. But this was a point that he was not willing to discuss in the presence of someone so lacking in the power to live as Dharma Das. The Dewan feared that Dharma Das would say that he, of course, understood the meaning of life, and then it would turn out that all one had to do was to love man and God. Of course one had to, but that explained nothing. So the Dewan was trying to think of something that would completely alter the course of the conversation.

Just then a secretary came in and said that Raja Muzaffar Khan was on the phone. Ram Nath's face lit up. He rose quickly and left the room to take the call. Could this be an invitation to taste another slice of life at Adampur? He quickened his pace as he thought of that possibility.

But the Raja merely wanted to ask the Dewan for a little advice. He was in a very awkward predicament. The Government had asked for the loan of his Adampur estate, which they wanted as an internment camp for some of the arrested leaders; the jails were full, and place had to be found for those who were being arrested each day. Simultaneously, the Congress Party workers had asked him for a donation toward the expense of medical treatment for the injured poor. The Raja said he would like to say yes to both sides; that, he said, appealed to his sense of fairness and was also the wise thing to do. One never knew which way the future would go. But as he did not feel that he could give up his estate, he thought he should refuse both requests. He asked what the Dewan would advise.

Ram Nath tugged at his beard. He realized that the advice he was about to give took into account his own desires for the future, but he thought it was also shrewd and equal to the requirements of the situation.

"Raja Sahib, you must not let these people get their knife into you, and yet you have your own interests to consider. Give the Congress people some money. Tell the Government that your health constrains you to spend some time on your estate, but, because you realize that they must be helped at this difficult time, you will be glad to place at their disposal your house at Mussoorie."

The Raja was delighted with this advice. "Excellent idea, my friend, excellent idea! I do not want to go to Mussoorie this summer, and your suggestion will enable us to keep the Adampur estate for our delightful visits there. I can see you are a far-sighted man, Ram Nath. We must go there as soon as I have cleared up this situation." And he rang off.

Ram Nath felt as if he had been hit in the solar plexus by the insinuations of Muzaffar Khan. The Raja was utterly shameless about these things—and he was always so accurate. He had immediately realized that, in giving his advice, Ram Nath had wanted to keep the door open for visits to Ranu and her friend even though he tried to give people the impression that he was much too disciplined and clean-living a person to indulge himself in that way. The Dewan truly wished he could give up his double life and be just an admirable person, but every now and again he felt that he had to go out and taste more fully the life of the senses which had been denied to him. It was too late to hope that his wife could give him what he wanted, so he told himself it was excusable that he should go out on his own. He wished he could make a clean breast of this to someone who would understand his problem. Geeta perhaps would—but it might also shock her.

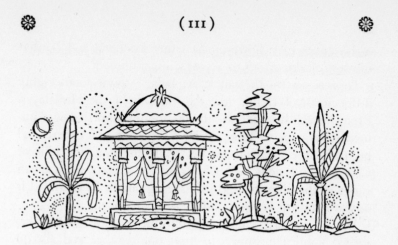

CHAPTER SIXTEEN

LENA AND JAI, and a score or more of their companions, were charged before the District Magistrate with having disobeyed the proclamation against the holding of public meetings. None of the accused took any part in the trial: all through the proceedings they stood silently in the dock of the improvised courtroom within the walls of the jail. This exasperated the Magistrate, who prided himself on being exceptional among the English for his sympathy toward the aspirations of the people of India—which he naïvely understood to be a desire on their part to hold more of the important governmental appointments and to be admitted to the British clubs. He had recently been posted to Delhi because it was felt that he would create an air of benignity in the trial of these cases, and it was expected that he would follow the directive of the Administration, which prescribed six months as the normal punishment for the accused. Because of his annoyance, however, he sentenced Lena and Jai and the rest of the group to a year's imprisonment.

Jai was sent to the jail at Ambala, a town about eighty miles north of Delhi, near the foothills of the Himalayas. From his cell he could see the mountains, and that was immediately a joy to him. For the last four years there had been no time for visits to the family home in the hills of Chamba. But now he could trace the distant Himalayan range in the distance, and in his imagination he extended it onward toward Kangra and then to Chamba.

He did not lack companionship, for the jail manual permitted political prisoners to meet one another and also to talk to the good-conduct prisoners from the other sections of the jail. And Jassa Singh, his warder, an immense Sikh who always wore a black turban that gave his cruel face a sinister look and a certain air of mystery, was extremely kind to him. In spite of Jai's protests, he insisted on bringing him savoury Punjabi dishes. But there were several new circumstances to which Jai had to become accustomed. There were no books, and for the first weeks no letters could be received or sent. Later, permission was given to receive letters once a week, visitors once a fortnight, and certain books.

Meanwhile, Jai found himself trying to assess his own life. As he looked out at the hills, the Himalayas seemed to break through the brittleness that had settled in him. The mountain view was the first intense experience of natural beauty which he had had in years, and he could feel the great sky-touching hills breaking through the drought within him and replacing it by a sweetness that melted within him. The experience surged through his being, and he felt the tears rise in his eyes. He was washing out the accumulated dryness in him. He realized that he had allowed himself to be narrowed by complete absorption in political work. Something had gone wrong. It was not that the Freedom Movement was restrictive. On the contrary, he recalled vividly the way it had taken and opened him out to beauty, to people, to ideas, to the tradition of the country and the exciting feeling of the future coming alive. He had learned to practise consideration of others, to be patient, and to maintain his equanimity with people at all times, no matter how trying the circumstances. But all this was becoming too mechanical. Now he realized that his own personality was shrinking because he was not giving it time and spaciousness. If he allowed himself to go on this way, it could be that, abstractly, he would practise all the virtues, but his contact with people would become wafer-thin and cold.

He thought also of his mother's guileful attempts to rescue him from too much preoccupation with the political movement. At the time, he had been able to get his mother to see his point of view and he had had no doubt at all that he was in the right. He blushed now at that sureness, and it made him feel very foolish. Now he realized that his mother had been wanting to fill him again with the sweetness of life from which he was withdrawing. At last he was able to laugh at himself. He felt like a boy learning how to balance himself on a bicycle. The sensation of falling made him feel helpless, but the smack against the earth brought quick relief and just a little hurt. He wanted to try again. It was an exciting feeling: wanting to try and yet be relaxed, to try and yet not try.

For want of writing equipment, he started to write verses in the sand outside his cell, with his finger. They were simple lines that flowed out of all that was happening within him. Yet it was exciting to gain this new dimension of expression. Soon he found another current entering into his poems. He realized that he was writing both about his longing for and his ambiguity about Lena. He deeply admired her seriousness and devotion to the Movement. Indeed, so strong was his feeling on these scores that he thought that to be moved so deeply was surely to love a person, and yet there was something lacking for which his being yearned. He did not want to take Lena away from the Movement, which was also so important a part of his own life, but he wanted her to pour warmth into him. He wanted to fill her with a deep tenderness which would remain with her while she worked and which would guard her from the dryness that seemed to infect the air.

A troubled feeling arose within him. Suppose Lena failed to satisfy his yearning. Suppose she did give him her love and still the yearning in him continued. What guarantee was there that she could fill the emptiness within him? Surely love must be like an inexhaustible mine so that, taking from it, with the aid of the beloved one, each moment of living would be lifted and sweetened. This was an awesome prospect of endless beauty, and he wondered—could Lena give this to him? Could anyone? And was love necessary? People seemed to get along without it, in a way, and yet they seemed always to be looking for it.

When he was able to push aside these speculations, there remained with Jai the taste of that late afternoon in his room when he had held Lena. It was the most vivid memory of his life. In a curious way, it seemed to provide the answer to his speculations about love. It was like a recurring beat in his system. He could no more forget it than go toward it. It was there, and he realized that he would have to submit to it. He would have to do as it dictated—it had already become the main theme of his writing and the obsession of his thoughts.

Jai felt that, for many of his colleagues, being locked up was a halting-point in their lives. Not that they regretted what they had done—none of them did. But they were like people who had been asked to wait until some great decision had been made.

For Dev Raj, who was one of them, this was not the case. He was a cousin of Munshi Ram, the young landlord of Delhi who had been killed on the day of the protest meeting against the arrest of Gandhi. In appearance he bore no resemblance to his cousin. He was tall and wiry, his thick head of hair was turning grey, and his keen eyes and rather fine features indicated a determined personality. But it was not his appearance that gave him any particular distinction. What Jai noticed in him was a certain air of completeness. In a material sense, he stood to lose more than the others. It was likely that part at least of his property would be confiscated to meet the considerable fine which had been imposed in addition to his being sentenced to imprisonment. With Munshi Ram dead and himself in jail, there was no knowing what might happen. In spite of these unpleasant prospects, Dev Raj seemed completely at ease in his new surroundings. He alone seemed without any tension. He would eat the simple bread and lentil ration of the jail with enjoyment, and each morning he would sit in a corner of the small courtyard rapt in contemplation. He always managed to look clean, and there was a smile on his face when he spoke to his companions or to the jailers.

Jai and Dev Raj respected each other's need to be alone, but they quite naturally found that for part of each day they talked of things they wanted to clarify—except that Dev Raj never seemed really in need of clarification. He seemed to be in a position of clarity and equilibrium at all times; yet he was always willing to consider the possibility of another position, and frequently he would seem to abandon his own. For example, Jai asked Dev one day what it was that he did each morning when he sat very still for about an hour.

"Oh—meditate, and I suppose I worship God," was Dev's reply.

"But what is your God?" asked Jai.

Dev looked at him for a few moments while he said nothing, but his eyes—always wide and clear—filled with a special lucidity. "It's quite clear. You don't need me to tell you. You know as much about God as I do," was his reply.

Jai smiled. "But I don't know about God at all."

Then Dev was serious. "You know, you really do know about God. What you reject or do not acknowledge is the God of your ancestors. But that only means that you are making contact with God in your own way. That, indeed, is what we are told to do in the Upanishads and in the Gita. You, Jai, are a Vedantist," and Dev Raj smiled teasingly at Jai.

Jai had always assumed that since he had put aside the ideas of religion in which he had been brought up, he was no longer a religious person and certainly hardly a godly one. He tried to explain this to Dev, who still thought he was wrong in his estimate of himself. "You are again assuming that because you have abandoned the way you learned in your childhood, you are an irreligious person. I can assure you that, from all I have seen of you, I would say you were definitely a religious person in the purest sense of the word. You are always trying to work out your own way, and you never aim at advantage to yourself. You are always working for the whole as you see it."

"That is probably somewhat overstated, but, assuming it is what I want to do, I do not see how it makes me religious," said Jai.

"Then this is largely a matter of words. You consider me a religious man. At any rate, I myself would say that I was, and, by my standards—which are presumably the standards of a religious person—I think you are one, too," explained Dev, smiling.

Jai, too, smiled. "Then there is very little I can say. You claim me as one of your kind, and how am I to say that I am not? But still I do not see how God comes into this."

Dev pondered over that a little and shrugged his shoulders. "You may be right. Perhaps He does not come into it. But, you see, when I try and straighten things out for myself, it is part of the process to reach out to the widest possible extent—to stretch out till I am taking into account not only the sentiment but also the intimations, intuitions, and the whole stillness which seems to be beyond me. As this process goes forward and touches the farthest limits, I feel it brings me right up against something primordial, and this experience I choose to call contact with God. You can call it something else, if you like."

They were both silent for a few minutes. Then Dev smiled very warmly, his bronze skin sparkling, and said: "Perhaps, like Buddha, we shouldn't talk about God in this world where we have to live within the limitations of a transient scheme of things. Perhaps at best we can be conscious of occasional enlightenment."

As a result of his talks with Dev, Jai became more free in

his own speculations. Time to look at himself—he realized how important this was, and he wondered at himself for having neglected it so completely these last few years. Had this been due to youthful personal arrogance? he asked himself. Had he allowed himself to think he had progressed far enough to forget about these things? He didn't know. But now he was stirred by, and enjoyed deeply, the process of coming to life again.

It filled him with joy that his desire to write poetry seemed unending. At times the impulse was so overpowering that he would write the whole morning and then would tear himself away so as to give some time to other things. After a few months in jail he was permitted to write one letter a fortnight to his family and to receive a reply. He was able to write to them truthfully that he was not unhappy, that he was learning about life and, ironically enough, was freeing himself from many chains which he had acquired outside jail! His letters were warm and full of tenderness, so that his father and the others, while not always clear as to what he meant, were filled with reassurance. He was not permitted correspondence with his friends, Lena and Shabir. A rhythm of love for Lena continued, though at times it seemed to become very tenuous.

At the end of November the British were negotiating a settlement with Gandhi and they began to release batches of prisoners taken during the Movement. There seemed to be no system determining the order of release, and Jai found himself in one of the last lots to be given their freedom. His father had heard that he had been selected for release and was waiting for him at the gate of the jail. Jai went with him to the village, where he spent most of that winter.

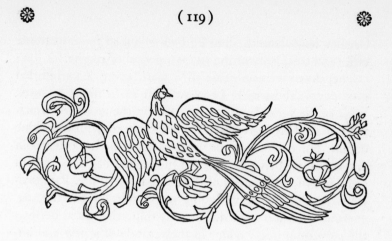

CHAPTER SEVENTEEN

WHEN THE Magistrate was pronouncing sentence of a year's imprisonment, Lena was looking at the lean arm of the constable who stood by her to keep her in custody. It was a very thin, underfed arm on which the veins stood out like fat worms. She shuddered a little with pity and then glanced at the man's face. It was glazed, almost lacquered, and his eyes looked as though they were part of the dirty white of the lime-washed walls of the room. He was obviously terribly bored with the whole business. It had put a stop to his life, it seemed to Lena, while she herself felt as though what was happening was all very necessary and real. As the sentence was announced, she cheerfully put out her hands for the manacles to be placed on her wrist. The constable with the lacquered face clipped them on with his emaciated fingers. It all seemed mad-house right to her, and as she was being driven to the women's jail—about half a mile down the circular road from the Red Fort—she looked forward to the quiet and simplicity of the jail as a period of respite.

The closed vehicle came to a stop before a two-storied mud-plastered barrack. Lena was led up a flight of brick stairs to the veranda on the upper floor, the arches of which were shaded by heavy reed drapes surfaced with deep-blue denim. The coolness of the veranda, after the hot courtroom and the stuffy drive, heightened the feeling of release which Lena felt in anticipation of this period of jail life. Paradoxically, imprisonment was going to provide for her the spaciousness that she wanted. The only thing that irked her was the pervading heavy odour in the veranda of a new and unfamiliar uncleanness, which during her stay in the jail she came to accept as the special mark of the over-all indignity of the situation.

Lena heard voices from a room off the veranda. One strain in the sound was familiar. She was led into the room. It was square, about twelve feet each way, with a barred medium-sized window in the back wall. The walls were bare and white-washed, relieving the oppression of the dull-grey cement floor. There was a simple string bedstead in one corner, on which sat her mother. A small table, two straight-backed office chairs, and a small cotton sitting-rug next to a low writing-desk in the corner opposite the bed completed the furnishings of the room. A pile of newspapers and a few books lay beside the desk.

The satisfied expression on Shanti Devi's face changed to a heavy, smiling seriousness when she saw Lena enter the room. The khaki-clad figure in front of her responded by turning around and smartly saluting a greeting to Lena. Lena tried to smile, but instinctively froze at the sight of the uniformed figure. The man in uniform waited, painfully conscious of her dismay. Then he cast a hopeful glance in the direction of Shanti Devi, who now said, putting her hand out to Lena:

"You look well, dear child. Come—and this is Major Ivor Jones, the superintendent of the jail. He is very kindly arranging to have another bed brought into our room. He has been so helpful to me." And she looked at the Major, the satisfied expression returning to her face.

Lena looked again at Major Jones. He bowed a little and smiled. He had a red, rather round face, slightly curling red hair, and a thick neck sprouting from his open collar. He was ugly, but his grey-green eyes twinkled with a friendly brightness and there was no hardness about his full lips. He wore immaculately pressed khakhi shirt and shorts, a regulation Sam Browne belt, thick fluffy woolen stockings that were folded over under his strong bare knees, and reddish-brown suede shoes, which were then the mark of the Country-Gentleman-British-Officer-in-India.

Lena smiled and, nodding quickly, said very properly in her beautiful melodious voice: "How do you do—I am glad to meet you."

The Major, feeling now that he was in the way, and that he must therefore retreat quickly if he wanted—as he did—to come and visit again with these strange and charming people, began to move toward the door, saying in quick, rapid-fire sentences, his eyes twinkling all the while: "I so much respect your dear Mother"—and he bowed to Shanti Devi. "You will be comfortable Miss Lena, if I can help it. Of course, not what you are used to, but we'll do our very best. Count on me, ladies," and he saluted and left.

As the sound of his footsteps faded, Shanti Devi smiled, her body wriggling a little as she said: "He's a very good friend, that man."

Lena didn't quite understand the import of this remark, and she still stood there, unthawed and strange. Shanti Devi quickly brushed off her smile and, getting up from the bed, she came up to her daughter with genuine love and concern showing in her face.

That whole day they talked of the Movement, their friends, Pandit Dharma Das, the servants, and the garden. Shanti Devi tried to enquire about Lena's friends, wondering whether her daughter had met any of special interest and hoping, while she enquired, that she was no longer reveal- ing her own pleasure in her friendship with the Major. But on this point Lena was silent and said nothing about Jai ex- cept that he had been in the group arrested with her.

Usually Shanti Devi fussed a great deal over her child, and generally Lena managed to tolerate this form of motherly solicitude. Now, in the closer confinement of the jail, she found it more difficult to bear. There was but this one small room and part of the veranda, and in the cool of the morn- ing and evening they could walk in the yard. Each day Shanti Devi's fussiness became more intrusive, and Lena found the growing strain almost unbearable. She began to find excuses not to be with her mother, and soon the two were seldom in the courtyard together; when her mother suggested a walk, Lena would say she had reading or other work to do. She even stayed in the unpleasant bathroom as long as possible, and encouraged her mother to take Major Jones out to the veranda on each of his regular morning visits. Shanti Devi seemed glad enough to do this, and Lena would often hear

the sound of laughter coming from her mother as she talked
to the Major.

From the first, Major Jones had been impressed by the dignified, portly but handsome Shanti Devi. He had gradually
found out more about her—that she was rich, respected, and
influential. He cast his mind back to his own country, England, and tried to make comparisons. He could not imagine
anyone there, in Shanti Devi's circumstances, voluntarily giving up all she had and going to jail for a cause. Also, he found
her warm and charming, so that his visits increased in fre-
quency and he looked forward to them, his thoughts becoming more and more preoccupied with her. For the first few
days he talked to his wife about Shanti Devi, but soon he realized that this had better cease, for Brenda, his wife, could
only conclude that he seemed to think of little but the new
inmate of his prison!

But now Ivor Jones was reluctant to have his visits take
place on the veranda. When he first saw Lena entering her
mother's room, her face clear, her lips shapely and perfect
for her oval face, her dark eyes flashing yet quiet and calm,
and carrying herself with the poise of a woman from Rajas-
than used to balancing several water jugs on her head, he
thought a goddess of the Hindus stood before him. He
wanted to share his rapture with someone. But with whom?
He dared not breathe it to his wife, Brenda.

Each day he came now to visit the mother and daughter,
hoping for an opportunity to see the young girl again. What
was it she had? Only strangeness, only the unexpected, he
told himself. He was pleased with himself for being so ra-
tional, and at times, as he went on his rounds or sat in his
office, he would feel that he had resolved the whole situation.

Then again, unbidden, the urge to see the girl would beat up the tempo of his very being; and so, in spite of himself, each morning he arrived at their room in something of a flutter. And each day he was left in a state of tension, for already the routine of talking with Shanti Devi on the veranda had become established and he hardly ever caught so much as a glimpse of Lena. It became more and more urgent for the distraught Major to put his feelings to the test. But meanwhile he realized that another serious barrier had presented itself: each day Shanti Devi seemed to enjoy his company more than ever and obviously wanted him to herself.

While Major Jones manfully fought the mounting frustration that had become the pervading influence of his life, Lena too was finding her frustrations becoming intolerable. For a variety of reasons, including her need to assure Lena that the girl alone was the focus of her life—and that Ivor Jones had not entered into it at all—Shanti Devi continued to fuss over her incessantly. Gently, Lena tried to tell her mother that she needed peace and quiet, and she hoped that by choosing her own time for her solitary walks in the courtyard and by remaining indoors when the Major called, she could demonstrate to Shanti Devi the nature of her real desires and needs. But no, her mother's zealous motivation was deep within her and their daily brief separations only redoubled her ardour for the rest of the day: or so it seemed to Lena.

Lena looked for some relief from this situation. She hinted at the possibility of another room for them. Perhaps Shanti Devi could mention it to her good friend the Major? But her mother seemed unwilling to understand.

Meanwhile, Ivor had not been idle. He had made a careful study of the activities of the two women throughout the day, and now he knew that at a certain hour in the morning and again in the early evening Lena was alone in the room. One morning he first visited at the usual hour and then returned when he knew that Lena would be alone. He knocked and waited. Lena came to the door. Ivor had done his utmost to steady himself for this moment, to infuse into himself a skeptical attitude and a general detachment. When he saw Lena, his hand went to the brim of his peaked cap in a smart salute, and in those few seconds all his defences crumbled. He felt that he was standing to attention and pledging his adoration, his fealty, his courage, his very manhood to this beautiful creature.

He stammered out an excuse for his second visit of the morning. He had not asked Shanti Devi whether her daughter was comfortable and now he was happy to be able to ask her personally.

Lena felt the great need of her life rushing to her tongue. It was impossible not to tell the friendly Major. She flushed a little, looking lovelier than ever, and her eyebrows rose archly as she said: "Well, since you have so kindly asked . . . this room, this very nice room, is really meant for just one person, isn't it? I mean, my mother was in it alone?"

The Major did not quite understand what she was getting at, but in his trained military way he replied quickly: "Yes. Of course. She was here alone. And it is a very small room."

Lena smiled, for the conversation seemed to be taking the right direction. "That's just the point, Major Jones. Can't we have a little more space?"

The Major thought a moment. There was a larger room that was not in use, and he would have done anything he could to make the girl happier. "Yes, Miss Lena. There is a larger room. You both could move—today, if you wish. Yes, today!"

"But no, I don't want a larger room. Even a smaller one would do, but a room of my own. Near this one, of course," she added quickly, and her face again flushed, but anxiously now, as she looked at him appealingly.

Ivor Jones felt his heart beat quicken as she looked into his eyes. He made a supreme effort to steady himself. "Too good to be true!"—the reply formed in his mind and almost burst from his lips, but he checked it and aloud he said: "You mean you really want a room of your own? But of course! We have things stored in the next three rooms, but then there is an empty one just like this. You may have it at once. I will instruct my men to clean it out now, and in the afternoon you can move."

Lena looked again into his eyes, her own reeling with delight. "Oh, thank you, Major Jones, thank you!" she said, her hands gesturing a little to emphasize her words.

Ivor Jones felt a little more in control of himself now. His own eyes were twinkling happily as he said to the girl: "Come, let me show you the room."

Rapidly they walked along the veranda, and there, just as it right-angled to the north, was the room. It looked out on a different scape, and over the jail wall rose the tops of several tall trees. Lena was very pleased and said she would get her things ready at once. Knowing this to be her immediate intent, the Major left her at her door.

When Shanti Devi returned from her walk, she saw two neat bundles in one corner of the room. She looked questioningly at them, but before she could formulate any words Lena had excitedly told her all that had happened. She ended by reassuring her mother: "And you will be much happier. You will have this room to yourself and your visitors can sit here with you instead of meeting you on the veranda."

Shanti Devi fussed somewhat, but she had found the meetings on the veranda with Major Jones much more restricting than when he came to the room, and Lena's point about the visits could not but solace her inwardly. That afternoon Lena moved into her new quarters.

For Lena this was a return to life. That night she dreamed of a great flow of slowly moving, star-shaped wisps of brilliant colours—orange, green, yellow, violet, and red. Then she seemed to be swept by them into an unfamiliar place. It looked like the mountains of Almora, but it was springy and even to walk on. She started to run, passing the fitfully flying butterflies. Then she flung herself down to rest and there by her side was Jai. She drew away, but he put his arm round her and held her, and she was glad, smiling to herself. Then came a patter of raindrops, heavy and sudden. Two drops fell on her eyes and she was awake. A monsoon shower—the first of the year—was drenching the earth, and the sweet smell of the dryness rose to her nostrils. She inhaled it—the first sweet breath of air she had known since she entered the jail.

She planned the day, laying out books, papers, and writing-materials, singing to herself softly. . . .

There was a knock on the door. She looked up. Major Jones was saluting her. The other hand he seemed to be trying to conceal from her. He came in and held out to her a bouquet of brightly coloured zinnias. He looked redder than ever, and the twinkle in his eyes came in broken intervals, unsurely.

"For your new room—to brighten it up."

She took the flowers and put them in a glass. She expected him to leave now, but he seemed rooted to the spot. He was trying to tell himself that at least he must say something.

"You are comfortable now, I hope?" he asked, his voice dry and hesitant.

Now Lena could say something she really meant. "Yes, Major Jones. I am so happy here—strange thing to say about jail, but it's true. You are very kind," and she smiled at him, flushing a little.

Ivor was restored by her words. She had said she was happy. Should he tell her now that what little he had done was not out of kindness? Or could he tell her how beautiful she was, or how much he wanted to do for her, how much he wanted, wanted her! He was utterly confused, and the words that came to his lips were expressed in a fumbling way: "We know so little—I mean, I do. The two of you here in jail. I can't understand it." He shook his head sadly, and then went on: "You will help us understand? I will come and learn." He felt something within warning him to stop.

Lena's face was serious now and rather withdrawn. The man's uniform and the whole situation upset her. She wanted to help him understand, but her instinct told her that he must learn to read the events and not to probe her heart. But she couldn't say this to him. She nodded now, rather mechanically, while she raised her hands together in salutation to indicate quietly and gently that she expected him to leave. Sensitive to her feelings, he immediately saluted and left.

Now that she had the room to herself again, Shanti Devi's mind fussed in anticipation through the scenes she would enact with the Major. She placed one of the chairs next to the bed. Perhaps soon she could put her pillow in the far corner and sit up against it there, leaving the whole bed clear and inviting—of course, just so he could sit on the edge and talk. And then they would sit like that perhaps for an hour each day, and she would be able to say things about happiness and about human relations which she had never been able to discuss with her peremptory husband.

Ivor Jones knew that part of the price of his visits to Lena's room would be the continuance of his visits to Shanti Devi. That was clear enough, and on the first day she, too, was given a bouquet of zinnias so that if she saw the flowers in her daughter's room she would think he had sent them lest Lena should feel she had been neglected by him. That day the Major was able to relax and talk to Shanti Devi. He wanted to know about her family, but Shanti Devi kept herself the centre of the conversation and constantly overflowed the bounds of words into gestures, glances, sighs, and blushes about her own personal hopes and dreams. Again and again in the next few days Ivor attempted in vain to coax her gently in the direction he wished her words to take. To her, all these gentle pressures had but one meaning: he wanted her to bare her heart yet a little more.

Each day he called at Lena's room, and she came to regard him as a dutiful functionary whom she might treat as such. She smiled at him and thanked him for his solicitude, and then she would nod and her glance would beckon him away. She thought that his eyes were curiously sad and at times even hurt, but she felt hesitant about drawing him out.

Once she said to him gently: "Does your work upset you? You do work very hard."

He shook his head, replying quickly, the blush on his face and neck spreading to his bare forearms: "No, no. I like my work. It isn't that."

She looked at him questioningly. She did want to ask what, then, it was which so burdened him, but she checked herself, letting the question remain within her.

Saying no more, he left. But that day he was unable to talk at all to Shanti Devi. He couldn't even try to draw her out, and when he responded to her, it was in monosyllables. Shanti Devi was deeply hurt, but she was a proud Panditani and made no show of her feelings. He left her abruptly and she felt as if he had torn away part of something vital in her. She felt quite ill that afternoon. The next morning when he called, she revived somewhat because he was gentle, knowing that he had hurt her, and gave her much conscious attention. But the next day again the friendly Major's manner was abstracted and his feet shifted nervously, scraping unpleasantly on the cement floor. The meetings became briefer each day, almost at the expense of good form.

All that Shanti Devi had expected of life was being taken away from her by these daily subtractions from what earlier had seemed to develop between the Major and herself. She really felt that each day something was being surgically cut away. She became old and listless, and in a short time she even gave up her evening outing in the yard.

Brenda Jones was alarmed at the transformation in her husband. She knew that the jails were full, that the whole Administration was strained almost to the breaking-point, but at the Club she saw that the other Sahibs took all this in their stride. In fact, they drank harder, shouted louder at the Club servants, and guffawed at the silliest jokes. It was only Ivor who was dejected and furtive. She wondered whether perhaps he was really not equal to all this, not a "pukka Sahib" after all. She was losing caste in her own eyes, poor woman.

All this time Ivor was eating his heart out. Devoutly he prayed for a miracle. He even prayed to be transformed into an Indian so that he could share the life of the country if not of the girl who so exhaustively filled each moment and space of his present existence. He came to hate the Administration, the Club, and the whole scheme of things which he was expected, in his own station and in appropriate measure, to uphold. He had made little headway with Lena. But that no longer mattered. Just to see her each day—and now sometimes he looked in briefly on his evening rounds, too—was the daily flowering of a life that he felt had never before even known what love and beauty meant. He began to read the early poems of W. B. Yeats— a friend in Ireland had sent him a copy three years before —and he revelled in their glowing, deep-toned romanticism, which became part of the imprisoned secret life he now lived.

The Major's obvious adoration began to please Lena, but she took it to be the feeling he might have for a much younger sister or perhaps an elder daughter, for never in his behaviour did he give her any reason to think that a passionate yearning for her was consuming him. So, to Lena, the visits of the Major were pleasant but very minor interludes in the day. She was unaware of the connection between her mother's growing lassitude and the Major, for the latter still visited regularly with Shanti Devi. She was also oblivious of the effect her presence in the jail was having on Brenda Jones. Thus, amid the torture that was wearing down the other two women—her mother and Brenda—and the secret explosive tension that filled Ivor, Lena, who was the prime cause of these unhappy intensities, found her own life moving daily into the calm and peace she had hoped for. Although each day she gave some time to reading the newspapers and pondering over the fortunes of the Movement, she did not feel that, cut off as she was, she could allow a vicarious sense of participation in the affairs that had formerly completely absorbed her to continue now to be her main concern.

Lena found intensely exciting the process of wandering alongside her new self. She wondered why she had given no time at all to her study of classical music, which she deeply loved. And then, she no longer had any close friends. Only two or three years earlier there had been so much affection, fun, and adventure between her and at least two of her college mates. Now she had grown into a lonely corner of her own, it seemed. She smiled at herself for allowing all this to happen, and then somehow she felt like a diver poised at the end of a supple, high diving-plank from which she would soon plunge into life anew. It exhilarated her, this wanting again to be fully alive, and she felt ready for it now.

But in the prospect before her, something deeply disturbed her. Most of the follies of the last few years, as she saw them, she could smile at now, but her drawing away from Jai in the last few months before their arrest she could not understand or justify. The fact remained that she had withdrawn, and she had no assurance that when she plunged back into life she would find him again. Perhaps he would not want her after the way she had treated him, or perhaps her own plunge would take her elsewhere.

Toward the end of August, Shanti Devi's lassitude seemed clearly to deteriorate into illness. She was unable to leave her bed, and she ran a temperature. Lena and the Major now shared a common alarm on this account, and even this community of interest brought the demented man a deep feeling of satisfaction. He acted quickly and at the highest level. Colonel Smith, the leading Government doctor in Delhi, was brought in to see Shanti Devi. He was a gentleman of the old school. He came dressed in a well-cut tussah silk suit, and his white hair was immaculately parted in the centre and brushed with pomade till it shone. He took Shanti Devi's pulse, used his stethoscope, listened to her plaint, and then wrote out a prescription for a fever mixture that he said would certainly cure her. She shook her head and said she was very ill, but he was polite and firm and said to Ivor, as he left:

"Old pretender, your Panditani has probably had enough of it here and wants to get out again. Just you give her that mixture for two or three days and let me know."

Ivor and Lena were reassured by Colonel Smith's confidence, but the scheme of things was breaking at another vital point. That summer the wives of the British administrators had not gone to the hills, for there was intense fear that at any moment there might occur a violent uprising and it was felt therefore that the men and women should stick together. For Brenda, the long hot days, together with her husband's strange behaviour and the depressing fact that since early summer he had no longer behaved towards her as a wife was entitled to expect, had proved too much for her. She was very pretty and rather buxom. Men entering middle age found her quite devastatingly attractive. And during this period of dejection, while her husband was on his evening rounds, she had seen much of Harold Binns, the Commissioner—a bachelor of forty-seven, very handsome but rather taciturn. The comparatively young woman—Brenda was thirty-six—in the full bloom of her womanhood was irresistible to him. He decided that he needed affection and a home. He had never before felt so strongly about anyone. Brenda was finding in him all that her husband now denied her, and she liked his protective, definitive presence. Harold Binns had accumulated a sizable fortune, and he was due for a long leave at home in England. He now proposed to Brenda that they should go home on the same boat. On the pretext of visiting friends, she would go to Bombay, and from there they would sail together for England. Brenda left for Bombay on the day the doctor called to see Shanti Devi. At the railway station there was an affectionate farewell between Ivor and Brenda. She was to return in a fortnight, and Ivor hoped that during this period he would be able to make some headway with Lena. He was glad of this period of respite. He would now be able to go ahead with his own plans without having to face his wife's downcast presence at home.

For three days Shanti Devi took Colonel Smith's prescription, but she did not improve. Ivor telephoned the doctor, whose only reply was: "The mixture as before, the mixture as before, my boy, for another three days. She can't fool you longer than that!" After another three days her temperature was still running. She was becoming increasingly restless and had now developed a cough. Colonel Smith came again to see her. This time he spent an hour with her. In the course of his stay, he learned that her husband was known to be the cleverest lawyer in Delhi. He decided, not entirely on medical grounds, that it would be unwise for the Administration to keep Shanti Devi in prison any longer. If her condition should become really serious, her famous husband would certainly make capital of it against the Government.

He said to Ivor: "I was mistaken about her. She is very ill. Partly auto-suggestion, of course, but she is sinking rapidly. Must get her out before anything happens. Write a report and I'll countersign it immediately. And, of course, she will fret herself to death if her daughter remains in prison. Both of them must go at once."

Ivor was stricken as with forked lightning when he heard the last part of the doctor's conclusion. Instinctively he began to stammer an appeal to the doctor: "But—but—" He couldn't go on: it would make no sense. The sweat poured from his face, giving wordless expression to his confused despair. Colonel Smith looked at him searchingly for a moment, but decided to make no enquiries and walked away.

Ivor wrote up his report on the two inmates and sent it to Colonel Smith. Immediately it was returned, countersigned and marked for instantaneous action. Ivor forwarded it to the Inspector-General of Prisons, knowing that it would come back the next morning with instructions to release the prisoners. He drove home that evening without calling on Lena. In the empty house, he went from room to room searching for something that would give him support, meaning, and direction. But nothing helped—the house was as empty as he himself felt; he was like a straw in the wind. It was then that one of his messengers brought in a telegram. It was from Brenda. He read it over twice: "DON'T LET THIS HURT PLEASE. HAVE LEFT FOR LONDON WITH HAROLD. BRENDA."

He read the telegram again. Did it mean anything? Again he read it, but it was as though someone were reading it to a simulacrum. It meant nothing. He heard a breeze sigh gently through the trees in his garden. He listened intently.

The sound seemed to enter into him and he distinctly heard it in his brain like waves of wind scratching noisily through a field of withered yellow grass.

The next morning Shanti Devi and Lena were conducted from their rooms to a grey closed van and driven home. Both of them silently wondered what had become of Major Jones.

Part Two

CHAPTER EIGHTEEN

WRAPPED IN HIS thick quilt, Jai stood on the uneven brick surface of the eastern veranda on the second floor of his Harbanspura home. The stealthy early-morning air pressed two pillars of cold against his legs in their thin white cotton pyjamas; and though the rising sun's long fingers reached out and dazzled his eyes, his unshaven face goosepimpled uncomfortably. He had been awakened by the sound—unfamiliar now to his city-accustomed ears—of bullock carts crossing the open space to the east of the house. The piercing shrieks from the friction of the heavy unoiled parts would sink suddenly to a rich resinous bass and then climb precariously up again. And Jai still could hear the voices of the men urging on the oxen, pitched low but clearly audible:

"May a snake strike you! Dhi, dhi, dhi, ooo!"

"May your boat founder! Dhi, dhi!"

Jai looked down at the heavy, powdered earth over which

the carts had passed. The strip of rutted ground, which in his childhood had been the spacious scene of so many memorable games and titanic encounters, was no more than a narrow, scarred pathway.

Jai remembered the days and nights of his childhood in the village. In the summer they had slept on this very porch. Just beyond what had been their playground was a well, the waters of which were drawn by an ancient Persian wheel that was turned by an old grey ox, far into the evening. The wheel emitted the weirdest sound as the aged wooden parts of its gear jarred against each other. Over the well rose a dense neem tree that had grown to immense proportions, nourished constantly by the sweet waters of the well. As the sky darkened into night, the tree would seem to spread its immensity even farther; the creaking sound from the well grew macabre at this hour, and to Jai at the age of seven as he was ordered to bed, it was altogether a frightening ordeal to have to face. Each night was like an alloted vigil against the spirits of evil. Almost every night—or so it had seemed to him—he would wake at some mysterious hour and, after a supreme resolve, he would open his eyes slowly and fearfully peer in the direction of the tree to make certain it was not up to any mischief. Sometimes it would seem to him that his look had arrested it just as it was setting out on some evil design. It would be crouching ominously and then, very slowly before his eyes, it would resume its normal stance. Then Jai would recompose himself to sleep after committing his vigil to the brilliant and watchful constellations of unknown stars that had climbed into their stations in the secrecy of the night.

The memory of those childhood fears recalled to Jai that he had always found the village a little depressing. Harbanspura had meant something to him mainly because it was near the foothills—the quiet, ever-open gateway to the Himalayas, through which lay the roadway to the family summer home in the hills of Chamba. But now, as he stood on the porch, facing the rising sun, he was moved by the quiet rural scene.

While the village failed to draw him in an intensely personal way, Jai felt himself painfully aware of its appalling lacks and neglects. It amazed him that Harbanspura had gone on subsisting through scores of generations, facing crop failures, drought, unjust taxation, other exactions, and disease—subsisting without any evidence of help, it would seem, from the preserving arm of Vishnu.

How long, Jai wondered, could these wonderful feats of perseverance continue? It was true that, in spite of the unbroken sequence of hardships, the people still had an eagerness for life and the vitality to respond to it; and now there was perceptible among them a strong feeling for something better than the last few generations of implacable deterioration. Jai noticed that now, when the District Officer of the Imperial Raj and his minions visited the village—as had long been the custom—most of the men hung back, remaining in their mud houses or in the fields, for they resented the patronizing interest of the Administration's satrap in their affairs. They knew that this interest was directed at preserving intact the crushing weight of the feudal structure, the very existence of which was precisely what most of them bitterly resented.

All this came out in what the young men said to Jai. He talked with them a great deal. Some of them had been to school, but, educated or not, they all seemed to be groping for some widening of their horizons.

"Well, why don't we do something about it? Things don't just happen by magic," said Jai.

Desa Singh was a burly young Sikh farmer who had returned from high school a few years before. He had a pleasant, round face the colour of mottled ripening tomatoes. He looked like a reservoir of power, but, in a way, he was typical of the general inability to tap that power. Smiling slowly, he pulled at the sweet grass growing where the group sat and, munching a stalk, he said: "Jai Singh, how can anything be done here? Look at Kharak Singh, the headman of the village, and Baba Tehl Singh, and others. They dominate the panchayat and they think they are in league with God or the Guru. They even think the rain comes because of them. Would they let us do anything? . . . No, there's no hope till those ancient trumpeteers fall down dead—and I am beginning to doubt that they ever will." And Desa stretched his sensuous arms as if he wished all this dull stuff were over and they could talk about the young women instead.

But Pritam Singh, a wiry, dark young man who had not been to school but whose father had taught him Punjabi so that he could read and write fluently, had other ideas. He pushed back his turban and said in a strong, firm voice: "And what when they are dead? There'll just be another crop of hardy whitebeards in the field. It's not that these old duffers keep us from doing things, but they don't want things to get any worse, so they set themselves up as the defenders of what little we have. The real trouble is that we are up against it every day of the year. Always there's an emergency. Yesterday we lost seven head of fine plough cattle. They just fell down and died—foot-and-mouth disease or something. How is the ploughing to be done in time for the next sowing, I ask you? We haven't enough money in the village to replace them, without borrowing from that rascal Koshi Mall, who charges one-hundred-per-cent interest. And even if we did that, who in his senses would sell us any cattle now when all the farmers in the Punjab are about to begin their plough-ing? No, no one would even lend us a couple of teams of plough animals! So . . . you see, brothers, on our heads is always an endless crisis: unploughed land, less grain, less income with which to pay the land tax, the attachment of our farms, and, of course, less food to eat. Where does it all stop?" Pritam Singh's dark face had not hardened as he said all this; at the end of his explanation, his deep eyes were filled with sorrow, and yet he seemed strangely unperturbed.

Jai felt that there must be some way out of this endless cy-cle of despair. He was determined to explore the situation with these men. "But we must not let all this happen to us. Right now, what is the thing we need most?"

Pritam Singh reflected a moment. Then, nodding his head and gesticulating with his hands as if to indicate that the posi-tion was quite clear, he said: "Right now we must find a way to plough our land. We have heard of tractors—you feed them gasoline and they plough up the land. A tractor would save us now, but the nearest one is probably at Delhi. Then there's the Government Agricultural Department Farm at Gurdaspur. They must have at least ten surplus animals, well-fed and strong: six of them would save us, but those dogs would not let us touch their cattle."

If these were the only alternatives, then they must get the cattle from the Government Farm, thought Jai. But he wanted to find out what would happen after the ploughing, so he asked: "If we do find the plough cattle, or even a tractor, what then?"

It was Desa Singh's face which then lit up, and, in his

deep, rolling voice he gurgled out an answer: "What then, Jai Singh? Plough and sow the seed. Then we will dance and sing with the girls when the rains come. Jai Singh, the next thing is to get this chap, Pritam Singh, not to hide his sister. Yes, you wouldn't believe it—look at him!—but, by the Guru, his sister is the loveliest thing ever sent to Harbanspura, and Pritam Singh won't let her come out and join in the singing. What's wrong with us—aren't we men? And isn't she a village girl? Tell Pritam Singh not to spoil our summer sport. If he does, I swear I'll take his young she-goat into the fields with me."

They all burst out laughing at Desa's threat. Pritam Singh smiled. "The Guru knows whether Desa Singh's tongue is in his mouth or between his legs. The things that bastard says! Even my she-goat is not willing, Desa!"

Jai, too, laughed and, putting his hand on Desa's knee, he interjected: "I agree with Desa about the singing and dancing. We must all be there, including Pritam's sister. But I still want to know—what after the dancing?"

Someone said eargerly: "Then, more water. More sweet water to strengthen the seedlings which the rains will draw forth from the motherly earth. Water from an inexhaustible well, like the well at the Government Farm—they say it is worked by electricity."

Pritam Singh nodded and again pushed his rough white turban back. "Yes," he said. "Water, and a new well. Then leave the rest to us. We will have full, heavy harvests and we shall buy better cattle, and manure for our fields. Then, if their official eunuch-minded Government would only let us alone, we would build our own school, improve our mango groves, and dig ourselves a decent sanitary system like the

Government has for its minions in Delhi. Oh, there are hundreds of things to do, brothers."

The others nodded and murmured approval. They were already feeling hopeful. Desa Singh looked up at the sky. Over the distant mountains, a cloud was anchored. His big voice boomed again. "One more shower of rain and that wheat crop will be as full of weight and sweetness as I have ever seen. Then, boys, will we sing and dance at Baisakhi next month! Sweetness in the fields and more sweetness in our homes when we return from the fields. Beautiful-voiced sweetness is the thing for me! Jai Singh, this man Pritam's sister sings beautifully. Stay in the village awhile and, after the wheat harvest, let us all hear her sing. Stay, Jai Singh. Say you will stay!" cried Desa lustily.

CHAPTER NINETEEN

IN DELHI, Dewan Ram Nath was trying to learn the ways of a new era. He saw the solid order of things created by the British, which he had accepted as permanent, crumble before the 1930-1 phase of the national movement. Those years proved to him that nothing short of extermination could subdue the spirit of the people. In 1919 the British had tried shooting, brutal corporal punishment, widespread curfews, sentences of imprisonment for life, and confiscation of property. But the movement for freedom swelled into the alleys and villages, and in 1930, for all the effort of the great Imperial Government, there were simply not enough soldiers and policemen to cope with the mammoth processions, the picketing and meetings. So the British took all the leaders, all the workers, all those who might be regarded as troublemakers, and lodged them in jail. Hundreds of thousands were incarcerated, but each day the number of demonstrations increased. Thus, imprisonment and forced labour in jail also failed to quell the spirit of the people.

Ram Nath knew that for Britain now to undertake a fullscale military action against India was impossible. Besides, how undertake it? Gandhi and the other leaders were not offering physical resistance. To bring an army against them would have demoralized the men in uniform. Of course, Ram Nath had heard his friend Sir Robert Brick, the Home Member of the Viceroy's Council, talk boastfully about the power of the British Lion and what it could do. No one in India denied the power of the Lion, but, though Ram Nath never dared to contradict his friend, he knew that the man was talking nonsense. He asked himself, how could force be used unless there was a point of application where it could be effective? There was none in India—there was just mass awakened life and resilience.

It was through this flux that Ram Nath found himself having to pick his way. Early in 1933 his son, Dina Nath, came and said that admission at Oxford or Cambridge had to be obtained that year for two young men in the family who were due to go abroad to complete their education. When he heard his son's voice, Ram Nath was sitting on the lawn under a large garden umbrella that was tilted against the mid-morning sun so as to shade his face while the warm rays fell on his body and on his legs, which were propped up on a stool. He looked up, jutting out his little pointed beard, now completely white, in the direction of his son.

"*Hein?*" he said, his face wrinkling into a query. "Oxford or Cambridge? Nonsense, my dear boy! They can't go there."

Dina Nath always looked confused, though sometimes his large, smooth brow and his unexpressive eyes created the illusion of a man engaged in lofty speculation. Now he just did not understand what his father meant, and he looked more confused than ever. "But, Father, we have all been there. I—I just don't understand."

Ram Nath sat up straight. "Yes, you have all been there—God knows whatever for. But that's not the point. Don't you see that times have changed? Don't you see that now it is the techniques that will be wanted in our country? Don't you see that the people want to make things for themselves? Tell the young men that one of them will go to the Massachusetts Institute of Technology and the other to Munich. That is my decision."

Ram Nath was quite right. So right that the dejected Dina Nath, who took the message and thought he was going to receive black looks, discovered instead that the young men were immensely glad. They, too, though not so consciously as the old Dewan, wanted to learn something that would give them a footing in industry, mining, or trade.

But a much more serious matter had to be decided. It was becoming clear to Ram Nath that in the new era the tenants on his farms—who had been models of contentment and had won for him the reputation of an ideal landowner—would no longer agree to work on the basis of surrendering to the landowner a full half of the crop as rental. They would insist on keeping two thirds, and on marginal lands perhaps three fourths, of the crop. On ten or fifteen thousand acres of land, this decrease in rental would mean a steep decline in income, and that was a matter which would affect the whole family. Dewan Ram Nath was the head of the family and the manager of its affairs. It was within his competence to alter rentals, but that was not his conception of the enlightened pater familias. He decided to invite the whole family to spend the day at Dewan House, when he would tell them what was happening in the world and ask them to accept the changes that had to be made.

As was customary on these occasions, the "family" was construed to include the Dewan's sister's brother-in-law's son, his wife's cousin's husband's brother, and all those who could claim any relationship or connection with the Dewan. And it was understood that there would be an air of ceremony and dignity. All the men would be dressed in their best long coats and the women would wear silk saris, heavily embroidered with gold, and as much jewellery as they could carry. And, finally, the evening meal would be served in and eaten from silver dishes.

For days before the date fixed for the gathering, the Dewan spent all his time poring over his accounts. He revelled in the galaxies of figures yielded by the various possibilities that he discussed with his men. So many factors had to be considered. There was not just the isolated fact of the farm rentals. He had to take into account the steadily rising rentals from the city properties, and there was the additional income from the professions and the superior Governmental services into which many members of the family had gone. He had enquired into the matter, as he was entitled to do, and had been surprised by the affluence of many of the lawyers and doctors in the family. He decided that these people must be asked to put more of their income to productive use.

After looking at all the possibilities, Ram Nath came to the conclusion that, even after reducing the farm rentals, the family income could be increased. With a chuckle of pleasure, he imagined the surprise of the family when he would unfold to them his magical and masterful plans.

The day of the meeting arrived. All was resplendence and colour, and the servants were dressed in spotless white. In the morning there was no talk of business affairs. There were endless bits of gossip to be exchanged and boasts to be made of how well so-and-so's son was doing, or how excellent a marriage had been arranged. Also there was the delicate task of so arranging things that those members of the family who were not on speaking terms with one another were kept from situations in which their sharp silences could start a scene. And Ram Nath astutely calculated that after a good midday meal the tensions of propinquity would be lowered and business would be smoother. Many soothing and delightful dishes were to be served at luncheon.

Ram Nath was in very high spirits. He was elated by his secret good news for the family on an occasion when it had got round that hard times were ahead. He was seventy now, and his sprightly movements had become rather jerky. To the callow young members of the family—the lieutenants, the tennis champions, the gay young men—he cut an extremely amusing figure in his grey frock coat as he strutted among the young girls, telling them how beautiful they were. Then he smiled at the whole group and said out loud: "So much beauty, beauty. Yes, God has been very good to us." The wife of a senior judge, pock-marked and fat and decidedly not favoured by Lakshmi, beamed at him and smiled shyly, as if very glad to be included.

After luncheon the party broke up for about half an hour's rest. Most of the older members of the family found a quiet corner somewhere for a siesta that came easily enough after the rich food. The young men insisted on playing cricket and trying out a few new strokes in spite of the Dewan's announcement that to play a strenuous game immediately after eating was most unscientific. Meanwhile, the tables were cleared except for heavy platters of fruit—both fresh and dried—nuts and spices, and the delicate wrought-silver dishes heaped with the acrid pan leaf that all of them would want to chew to aid their over-taxed gastronomies.

The clan regathered, and Ram Nath opened the meeting.

"Kinsfolk, these are strange times, very strange times, and I knew we would all want to meet and face them together. I wish the other old families in the country were as sensible as we are. If they are not, they will be swept away, leaving neither name nor mark; but we do not intend to let that happen to us"—greeted with nods while the Dewan smiled. "The world is changing fast.

"I know many of you did not agree with me. But I had the fullest faith in the political wisdom of the British. I thought they would be able to reach an honourable settlement with the leaders of our country, but I admit they have disappointed me. Every day they make some silly mistake. It appears to me that they are building their own last road—and it is a road into the sea. I do not know what is going to happen, but we must not let the new forces overwhelm us. Why

should we be swamped? This is our country as much as anyone else's."

Ram Nath realized that many of those present were not
listening. The fools, he thought, they don't know anything
and don't want to learn. He straightened his small figure
and, pushing out his chin, boomed out: "I know you are
wondering what all this has to do with our property. But
that is just the point. If we can't see that there is a very per-
tinent relationship, we will blow up our estates and be left
standing on the ashes. Do we want that to happen? Of course
not. Then listen to me."

Ram Nath emitted a little grunt, feeling that he had made
his point. Then he went on with his previous thought. "With
great respect, and I do respect them, I do not know whether
Gandhiji—and more so that young man Jawaharlal—are
aware of what they are doing. Villagers and scavengers are
taking part in the national movement and are going to jail
with the best people. Are they going to work for us in the
old way? Then, what will we do? None of us can even hold
a spade. That is the point. Do you see it now?" And he nodded his head several times all round the room.

Dina Nath was very troubled by what he thought was
coming. Was his father going to say that they must sell the
land? Now thirty-nine years of age, Dina Nath had not yet
been entrusted with the management of the estates, but he
did go out and spend some of his time in the family villages,
where he was very happy. There everyone seemed to respect
him, and the only questions they asked were "Young
Dewan, what is the time?" or "Young Dewan, is England as
big as Delhi?" or "Is it true that, with just his staff, Gandhiji
is turning out the British?" And when they were very
friendly, they might ask: "Young Dewan, it is said the Eng-

lish women are fierce like men or as cold as fish—tell us, is that so?" Dina Nath loved all this. It never occurred to him that the more intelligent village people kept away from him and went about their work, regarding him as no better than a great nuisance. Anyhow, Dina Nath could not possibly see himself cut off from the land.

There were others in the gathering who would also have opposed stoutly any suggestion that the family estates should be liquidated. One of them murmured: "But, Ram Nathji, we must keep our lands. Land is permanent. What else is?" And the questioner looked at the rest of the gathering as if asking for their approval—which came in a chorus.

Ram Nath raised his voice. "Who said I was proposing that we sell our estates? I am not mad. Do you think that is the way I take my responsibilities as the head of the family —this great family?" And again the jutting chin sought the approval of the gathering. He felt that this was the time to tell them what wonders he was doing for them. He held out his right hand to his listeners and said: "I will increase your prosperity and you will not lose an inch of land. That is what I propose. But we must increase the share of the tenants from half the produce to two thirds so that we keep them on our side."

"But how will we live if we decrease our income? We must educate our children; we are always expected to subscribe to the homes for Brahmins and to political funds, and now the politicians are making us decrease rents. And they will also expect us to increase our contributions to them. They are a crooked lot," said the Judge.

"It doesn't help to call other people names, my friends. We must face the facts as they are. The tenants will go against us if we do not give them a larger share of the produce. But let me tell you how we will fare if we do this. Last year on the old rentals we found it very difficult to get any tenants for our land by the river, so I gave four families two thirds of the produce. Do you know what the result has been? On these lands the yield has gone up by at least thirty per cent. Do you see? So that half the loss of rent has come back to us. Now, if we decrease all our rents to one third, we can count on a twenty-five-per-cent increase in production, which means that half of what we give away we will get back. But how do we make up the rest of our loss? You all know that five hundred acres near Nurpur for which we have never been able to get any cultivators on the half-and-half basis of produce-division? Well, at the new rental we will be able to get tenants. I have already made enquiries. And as it is very good land, the third rental there will be almost equal to the half-share rental which we are now getting from our other lands. So you see, this, together with the increased production on the other lands, will make up our income from three thousand acres to its present level. What do you think of that? Isn't it worth doing? Tell me!"

"Yes, Dewanji, that sounds right, but suppose there is no increase of production on the land, and, in any case, how do we make up our income on the rest of our five thousand acres?" asked one of the lawyers in the group.

Ram Nath looked at him coldly. "You lawyers never believe any evidence that the other side produces! In two separate areas, four families are producing at least thirty per cent more crop on the lower rental. The old rent is so high that there is not enough incentive to the cultivator to produce more. Now, because he will keep two thirds, he will work really hard. I have said the crop will go up by twenty-five per cent, but it will probably be more than that."

"But what about the loss on the income from the rest of the land?" persisted the lawyer.

Ram Nath smiled. "Fortunately, not all the forces in the new India are unfavourable to us. The cities and towns are growing rapidly. The value of our urban land is increasing. Our rents in the city are absurdly low. I am going to put all of them up by twenty-five per cent. Let me tell you, there is nothing immoral in all this. The shopkeepers and, as you know, the lawyers and doctors are making good money. We will take more from them so that the people in the villages, who have so little, may have more. We will just be a catalyst —a catalyst, you understand"—and he looked around, hoping that they understood the word. "Of course we will not suffer—why should we?" Ram Nath grunted with satisfaction, and then he smiled and sat down. He was very pleased with himself. The moral argument had occurred to him as he was speaking, and it seemed to him such a good one.

Ram Nath expected immediate applause, acclamation— something to indicate how splendidly he had done his task. But, instead, each man in the group now turned to his neighbour to discuss the position. Ram Nath looked at them all coldly. How could he have thought of them as good-looking? he asked himself. They were a bunch of overfed, greedy people. It showed on their faces. Why had he bothered with them at all, the idiots? He was the head of the family, and he should have done just what he thought fit.

He noticed that some of the younger members of the group were pleased that the meeting seemed to be over. They had not come there to discuss business affairs. There, at the back of the room, he saw a Captain obviously flirting with a beautiful cousin of his. Ram Nath was not upset. He immediately wished that Geeta had been there. He sighed and looked away into the distance. How empty and futile had been all this talk of figures and income! None of it mattered. Life was meant to be the beautiful thing it became when Geeta was there. The people in the room looked uglier than ever. He sat with his chin in his hand and his elbow on the table. With his other hand, he started to tap the table, making his impatience quite clear. He wished that this was all over so that he could return to his room. There he could think of Geeta, and even of Ranu. Why didn't he just walk out now and do that? Why sit here any longer?

At that point, his son broke the silence. "Father, why can't we increase the city rents and leave the farm rents as they are? Then we would be much better off."

Ram Nath was amazed. His face shot up, his eyes blazing at his son. Here was the man he had spent a small fortune on trying to educate, and he clearly had not understood the logic of the arrangement. For a moment Ram Nath was on the verge of bursting out at Dina Nath, but then he half closed his eyes and, leaning his face on his hand, said very quietly: "Doesn't matter, son, don't worry about that. I'll tell one of the managers to explain it to you."

Dina Nath remained standing there for a moment, looking rather dazed, and then his slow, corpulent figure sank again into the comfortable chesterfield.

But this was more than Ram Nath could take. Although he had controlled himself, he realized that he could not stand another minute of the meeting. God knew what rubbish these people might ask him. With a quick, jerky movement he got up and thumped the table.

"That is enough now. The meeting is over."

The fifty-three persons present looked up at him blankly,

not realizing what he meant. He nodded once, sharply, and walked out of the room.

In his own room he wondered at himself. He was seventy. He shouldn't give another moment to the affairs of the family. He was very rich. What was the point in worrying about a few rupees more or less? But what else could he do? Buy a small estate near Delhi and keep a mistress, like his bawdy friend Muzaffar Khan? No, that was not what he wanted, and he tried to brush aside the idea. But why not do it? Why not? And the idea suddenly became insistent. Already it seemed in his nerves, in his mind—everywhere. It need not fill his whole life—he could still have his books, and even his accounts if he wanted. Yes, he needed to add something to his life, not to renounce what he had. Of course, if conditions had been different, he might have tried to make a career in politics. But he was out of step with the Congress Party, and, in any case, he was too proud now to go over to them when it was clear that they were winning. So he would have to look for a different sort of "career."

If only he could live his life again with someone like Geeta! He thought of her dark, strong, and yet tender eyes, and his whole body yearned for tenderness. But, alas, all that had passed him by. He concluded that his "career" would have to be in the direction of that of his friend Muzaffar Khan. He smiled to himself and felt he had accomplished something in reaching this conclusion.

Just before the evening feast he emerged from his study. He was no longer thinking about the meeting and its absurd ending. He went up to the young girls. "Why," he asked, "tell me, why did you listen to all this rubbish today? You poor girls!"

A sharp, nervous-looking girl burst in: "But why pity us?

We listened more closely than many of the men. They try and keep us out of these things. Anyone knows that it is we, by our spending and saving, who control the family fortunes!"

Ram Nath looked at her and laughed. He wasn't really listening. But the talk of spending and saving reminded him that soon he would be spending quite a lot of money on his new "career." He hurried away from the girls lest they should somehow discover his thoughts. He thought of Geeta and wondered what she would say about his decision. He imagined himself explaining his plight to her, and he saw her smiling in reply and saying that she understood and that it would make no difference to her love for him.

He walked away from his guests, thinking of his own life. Was it moral for him to take a mistress? He tried to foster doubt, but the only answer that broke through was that surely it would be moral to do that which he deeply needed to do and from which he was excluded by his present life. Of course, it would be a pity to have to do it all so clandestinely, but to live with his mistress and to feel her tenderness would fulfil something in him and this might make him a better person. He smiled to himself. Again the moral argument in support of his decision—as it had done in the matter of the farm and city rentals—gave him a sense of finality.

After the sumptuous evening meal, everyone was tired and sleepy. They all got ready to leave and, coming up to the Dewan, they thanked him for his "masterly exposition" of the new situation. He was elated. After all, the day had been a success.

CHAPTER TWENTY

WITH THE HELP of friends at Gurdaspur, Jai was able to obtain from the Government Farm the loan of six plough cattle, and then from early in the morning till late in the evening the ploughing went on at Harbanspura. But before the dancing and singing festivals took place, Jai had to leave for Delhi. The negotiations between Gandhi and the British had broken down. The British were exasperated by Gandhi's insistence on certain fundamentals like a broad-based franchise and by his faith that, given responsibility, the people would act normally and sensibly. He had smiled and said to his British friends: "I thought they behaved quite well when they were belaboured and bayonetted by the police and your army—they never hit back. Don't you think then, if you decided to live at peace with them, you could count on their treating you well and respecting your interests?"

But the British naturally wanted all manner of safeguards for themselves and for those in India who had stood by them. And now they announced that the country consisted of scores of communities, such as the Moslems, Parsis, Sikhs, Christians, Jains, and so on; and also of many "interests," such as the landlords, the untouchables, the women, and the tribal peoples. All these they termed important minorities that stood in need of protection from the domineering Hindu majority. Again Gandhi smiled at them. He took down their own list of these minorities; for each he took the population figures and added them up. They came to more than the total population of India!

Little wonder, then, that for these and other rather similarly annoying reasons the British became very angry. This time, they decided, there would be no long-drawn-out recrudescence of the Movement. Without bothering overmuch about legalities, they promulgated ordinances giving themselves full powers. Immediately, all those who had recently been released were again apprehended. Each was summarily tried and sentenced to a term of imprisonment twice as long as on the previous occasion. Jai had been in Delhi only one day when he was arrested and sentenced to a two-year term in prison.

When Lena stepped out of the closed grey van on her release from her first prison term, she felt a sweetness in the air. There was Prahba, the gardener, smiling and thrusting a bouquet of roses into her arms. She looked up the flight of stairs to the front veranda of the house. Her father, standing there, was like an immense solidification of sadness. His moustache, which she had always remembered as bristling and very military, now drooped and slouched over one side of his mouth. To her, he had the appearance, not of a person standing and waiting, but of something that had been propped up there and left. But in spite of this pitiful sight, she couldn't help smiling at him. She knew somehow that it was the right thing to do. She ran up the stairs to him.

"Father!" she exclaimed. "Don't look so sad! Here we are, back again, and Mamma will soon be well," and she put her arms around his neck.

Then the thing at the top of the stairs came to life again. Even the slouching moustache seemed to bristle a little, and the corpulent figure became tremulous with the invigoration of the impact Lena made. All her life she had been remote from her father, regarding him as part institution and part unction. Now, standing there, holding and shaking her with his fat hands, he was excessively human. At this discovery, more joy and more sympathy for him overcame her. She smiled again at him, her eyes lighting up in a blaze.

"It's wonderful to be home again," she said. Then, looking at the inviting lines of the rattan veranda chairs, which before she had scarcely noticed, she added: "I could sit here for hours drinking it all in!"

By this time Shanti Devi was struggling out of the van, and together they went down the steps to help her.

Later, in her room, Lena opened the window wide. The familiar sounds from the garden—the chirping of minas, the singing of the birds in the trees, the raucous jays and crows, and the rustling of the leaves—came hurdling in. She opened the door to the eastern veranda and sat on the steps, filled with the gladness of her homecoming. The bees darting from one little flowering spray of grass to another amazed her; and each blade of grass itself sparkled and coursed with green life. She went out on to the lawn and, bending down, drew her fingers lightly over the grass. The cool stubble traced a hundred sensations on her hand. She slipped off her sandals and walked barefoot, enjoying the feel of the fresh, prickly turf against her feet.

Returning to her seat on the steps, she felt life pulsating in her. Through her mind passed the recollection of her close associates in the Movement and of their activities together. Yes, that was important, but did they, the others, feel as she did now? Did they know this much wider, ever-expanding, intensely alive, fluid feeling that she was experiencing? A gentle shudder of fear that they might be missing all this passed through her body.

At all hours—in the early morning, at midday, at sunset, and then under the stars at night—she would go out on to the lawn, and each time she seemed to experience something deeper. She seldom left the place. There seemed no need to go out and meet people at this stage of her life when she was learning with wonderment the sensitivity of her own being to everything around her. Not that she avoided people. She enjoyed talking with those around her—her father, the maids, the gardener, her father's clerks, and sometimes even her relatives, whom she had previously avoided. But there was no need just yet for a closeness to people.

One afternoon in the late summer, as Lena stepped out on to the lawn, a young gardener's assistant, naked to the waist, his dhoti tucked up, baring his slender legs, was swinging his long, pliable cane switch through the overgrown grass like a scythe. His feet set widely apart, and bending down from the waist, the young gardener would draw his uplifted right arm as far back as his pliant torso would permit and bring his slender wooden scythe whistling through the straight stalks stiffly pointed to the noontide sun. Then, still bending, he would take a little hopping step forward, and after a moment's relaxation his body would curve into action again.

His beautiful moving body gleamed in the sun. Lena looked
at him, transfixed. When the man stopped to rest, it was as
though an elixir had been withdrawn from her lips. She
waited, each moment heavily threading up in her. He began
to move again, turning now in her direction; she could see
his face, intent and yet in repose, his muscles relaxed, and
his forehead wet. Her enchantment heightened as the beautiful figure approached her and she heard the switch whir-
ring with a musical resonance to the accompaniment of
the rhythmic movement of his body. She became aware of
an echoing quiver in her own young body and felt the spell
reaching to her fingertips. The man was now about fifteen
paces from her, and as he completed his swing she came
within his field of vision. He abruptly straightened himself.
Then his eyes seemed to take the measure of the distance between his lowly occupation and the young mistress of the
house. He seemed to decide that he was disrespectfully close
to her. Greeting her with a low bow, he turned and walked
slowly to the far corner of the extensive lawn and sat down
as if waiting for her to give assent to his work by moving off
his field of action. Sensing this, Lena began to pick her way
along the hedge to the flower garden beyond the lawn. But
the heavy scent of the flowers seemed to sting her roused
senses, and she made her way quickly to the house.

 She returned to her room and lay down to rest, but she
tossed on her bed and could only compose her body and mind
in parts. She decided that she would take a cold shower and
then perhaps she would talk to her father. He would soothe
her by mixing reminiscences with hope for the future and a
certain caution about the present, inevitably ending by saying that she ought to have more jewellery and finer clothes.
She would laugh and tell him that she was amply provided,

or perhaps she would let him follow up his plans and it would give her a feeling of the graciousness and bounty of life when he would later smilingly put in her hands a parcel which she would open to find a necklace, a jewelled brace-let, or three—for some reason there were always three—gleaming soft silk saris embroidered with gold.

She went to the bathroom and undressed. She was turn-ing on the shower when, swinging her head to one side to throw her hair off her face, she caught a glimpse of her out-stretched body in the mirror. The white of her arm and the curves of her body seemed to quiver. She turned to the mir-ror and stood in front of it naked. Yes, her body was quiver-ing and her skin was warm. She felt a tingle under her knee caps, and her face surprised her. She had never known that it looked so much a part of her body. There was a nakedness about the two sides of the face, and her lips were amazingly full. She blushed at herself. She swung her body around and pirouetted on her toes. Then she swayed gently; how lithe, how deft she could be! If she let herself, she could fly into space. A kind of urgency to let herself go buzzed through her head.

After a quick shower, she dressed in one of the silk saris that her father had given her. On her wrist she put a jewelled Rajasthani bracelet, and she had the maid bring her flowers from the garden to deck her hair. Then she went straight to the telephone and rang Dewan House. She asked to speak to Geeta. In answer to Lena's question, Geeta said that she was busy for the rest of the day. Lena hoped she would be asked to join in whatever was happening, but the idea did not enter Geeta's head and they arranged to meet the next morning.

When Geeta hung up, Lena felt a seething tension within

her. She did not think now that her father's slow, kindly talk could soothe her. Alone she paced about the garden in her finery. Gradually she felt calmer in the familiar friendliness of the garden. But after dinner, as she sat on the steps of the veranda, the evening air touched her with a subtle sensuousness and she wanted utterly to be with people, to be doing things with them, to talk and laugh with them. The air was like a shadowy person brushing against her and then tantalizingly gliding away into the night. She wanted the unknown person who had brushed against her. Her throat was bursting with the unuttered call to him. She ran from the steps and walked quickly out of the gate. The street was deserted. She ran along it, searching, searching. At the crossroads she looked down into Court Road, and there, in the distance, were the lights of the police station. She shied away from the sight and walked quickly home, still searching but irked by a sense of restriction. Back in her room, she stepped out of her sari and lay down, her heart pounding hard and her mouth dry. She could not understand herself. At last a feeling of helplessness came over her and she slept.

The next day she drove to Dewan House. Geeta had no idea why Lena was coming, but when Lena arrived very smartly dressed and wearing a beautiful old Jaipur enamelled ruby-and-diamond necklace, she had an inkling that something new was happening.

Lena, for her own part, could not help being somewhat furtive while she talked to Geeta. As casually as she could, she said: "It's so good to be out of jail and to be able to meet people. I mean, wouldn't it be fun to meet some people our own age?"

Geeta understood at once. She enjoyed having the other girl in her power. She still smarted with jealousy over Jai, who was still in jail, but now Lena was asking her help. She said tantalizingly: "They come round when they want to, you know. There's not much to be done about these things."

Lena was not going to beg for anything. "Of course. But I suppose I have been in jail for so long that no one even remembers me"—and she visualized the beautiful girl standing naked yesterday before her mirror.

Geeta knew several young men—army officers, wealthy young business executives, and others who were known only by their fast cars—who gathered for a drink at Maiden's Hotel before lunch. She looked at Lena as if sizing her up. Yes, she would make a hit all right, but Geeta felt herself so much the centre of that world that she could afford to take along a novice without any detriment to her own dominance.

She said: "Let's go and have a drink at Maiden's."

This was something Lena had never done, but she felt up to anything. "Yes, let's."

Lena drove. They were there in a few minutes and sat under a garden umbrella on the lawn. Geeta ordered coffee for herself and a cognac, which, to Lena's amazement, she poured into the coffee. Geeta shook her head and smiled. "Not for you just yet. Have a sherry." Lena had a sherry.

In a few minutes, four men had swarmed around and joined them—two army officers, Akbar and Prakash, another young man they all called Vicki, and a heavy-set, smiling businessman, Amrit. They all ordered whisky-and-sodas and looked very relaxed. Lena thought it all so debonair. She took a sip of sherry, and as she tilted the glass to drain it, her eyes looked up at the beautiful arjun trees and beyond them to the blue sky flecked with a few floating clouds. It all looked so beautiful, so utterly lovely. She wanted to say so to the others, but she blushed instead. They would think her so unsophisticated.

They smoked, they laughed, they talked—Lena couldn't quite make out what about, even though she joined in. Then they went in and ate lunch. They all continued to laugh and talk and sometimes became quite hilarious. Occasionally there would be an air of mystery, as when one of their party would call hello to some doubtful-looking foreigner who was passing near their table.

When the party broke up and Lena dropped Geeta, she could not tell why but she was pleased and relaxed. She threw herself on her bed with an Arnold Bennett novel and soon she fell sound asleep.

The next day one of the servants came round to Lena's veranda and said that she was wanted on the telephone. Lena hoped that it was Geeta. She wanted to meet her new friends again. She said: "Hello."

"Hello there—that was lovely fun yesterday. Do join us for lunch today."

It wasn't Geeta. Lena's heart leapt. She steadied herself, but she felt her body quivering. "Thank you, I'll come. Yes, twelve thirty. Thank you."

She put down the phone. She couldn't make out whether she had been speaking to Akbar or to Prakash. Both army officers talked exactly alike. "How absurd," she said to herself as she went off to change.

Lena was elated as she drove to Maiden's, but she couldn't make out just why. Geeta was already there and seemed to respond rather sulkily to her greeting. Then Lena knew: she was happy to be independent of the other girl. She had escaped, and Geeta apparently regretted it.

Again there was fun and laughter at lunch, and later they danced. Prakash—it was he who had called her—swept her around so deftly. She loved it all, but never really understood what the others said and what all of them laughed about.

About a week later Prakash again called her and asked her to go out one evening to dinner and to dance. She immediately thanked him and accepted. But how could she go? Her parents had not asked her about the lunch appointments because Lena had numerous political friends and for years now she had gone to meetings and confabulations. But in the evenings she had remained at home. Now she dressed and said nothing, but drove off rather early, thinking that would be the wiser course. She felt badly about the implicit deception, but decided that it was necessary. She drove slowly through the park and saw the bandstand where she herself had spoken—was it only a year ago?—to hundreds of thousands of people. The memory stirred her, but somehow it was unbelievable. She drove on, not wanting to dwell too much on those things, and she brushed aside, with a slight qualm, the thought of Jai which had been evoked by these surroundings.

The dancing was delightful, and Prakash was smiling and gentle at dinner. Now that there were just the two of them, she had to listen to what he said—when there had been a crowd around, she had only pretended to listen, treating it all as just happy noise. He told her about his horses, about his commanding officer, and then about his sisters, who were in school at Simla. There were light little bits of information, that was all: "My sister Mona is very pretty, but Sheila is very naughty."

Lena mostly listened and smiled, but she was happy being

with him and felt quite protective for some reason. He looked so smart and sophisticated, but when he talked he was as innocent as a child.

Then Prakash went away for a month's field exercises. Lena continued to go to some of the lunches at Maiden's, but she found that she missed Prakash more and more. Much of the time she wondered about him. It would be so pleasant and easy to live with him. They would have two or three children and life would go happily.

Prakash returned, deeply tanned and looking very healthy. Lena blushed when she saw him, but he let it go without comment—he was always courteous and rather conventional. Lena wondered what would happen next.

Three days after his return they had another evening together. Prakash held her close as they danced, and when they sat down to dinner he could only smile at her. Words were apparently unnecessary to him now. When he saw her to her car, she let him take her hand. He held it and looked at her very seriously. Then he said:

"I must come and pay my respects to your dear father and mother."

She nodded. He saluted and left her. He was so proper and unsophisticated. She liked this about him. It was all turning out so wonderfully easy.

The next day came the news that Gandhi's talks with the British Viceroy had failed. Two days later the British announced their new ordinances, and on the following day Lena was arrested.

It was natural that Lena, in her present frame of mind, should not want to go to jail. She hoped it might be a light sentence. Certainly since she had been released she had done nothing remotely political. When the sentence of two years was pronounced, she felt that she was being banished forever.

CHAPTER TWENTY-ONE

FOR THE early part of the summer Dewan Ram Nath and his wife went to the hills above the luxuriant valley of the Doon, which lies like a sheltered gem between the foothills of the Himalayas and the further outcrop of toy hills known as the Sivaliks. But the Dewan never stayed long in the hills. He became impatient for contact with his estate managers and secretaries; and though he maintained that he had the best men in the country, who could be trusted with the diamond mines of Golcunda, he himself never could trust them even with one season's rents. Besides, though he would not admit it, Ram Nath missed the ready-made audience he had for his dissertations on philosophy and science. No one in the hills was interested in these things. This upset the

Dewan. Why did people need a vacation from the serious and important things of life? He kept telling them that it was absurd, but no one listened. Everyone was going off for a picnic, or to dance, or to play bridge, or just to talk to friends. Then again, Ram Nath did not like the heavy monsoon in the hills. In Delhi it was different. With the rains, everything revived instead of drooping under the continuous deluge as in the hills.

But this year there was a new compulsion for returning to the plains. Ram Nath had been considering very carefully the question of acquiring a mistress. He wavered a long time before coming to a decision. Some days he would tell himself that he was ready for complete renunciation of the carnal life. He would smell the fresh morning air in his garden and tell himself that he had been a fool and a knave to allow himself even to think of hiring a woman to satisfy his carnal lusts. On days like this, at the midday meal he would wax especially eloquent. He would extoll the virtues of philosophy and tell the young people that if only he had paid more attention to becoming acquainted with the great thinkers of the past when he was young, his life would have been a much happier one. He would leave the dining-room and return at once to his reading, and sometimes he would put down some of his thoughts on paper, adding a little note at the end of the effusion to the effect that the manuscript was to be given to his son a month after his own death. Some of the writings were to be given to a nephew in the army, and there were also some for Geeta; but these were only a few short things that were written to describe the beauty of his garden when the chrysanthemums or the zinnias were in bloom.

The spell of dedication to these high pursuits would,

however, be unaccountably broken. The apparent course of events would generally be that one of Ram Nath's managers would bring up some problem and that would begin a new train of thought. The Dewan was full of the most weird apprehensions regarding the safety of his property. For nights he would lie awake or fall into an uneasy doze trying to set right in his mind certain doubts about the validity of the title deeds to some of his estates which had been a gift to his ancestors from the Sikh rulers of the Punjab. For years there had been rumours that the deed of gift was a forgery perpetrated by his great-grandfather, who had held an unimportant position on the personal staff of a Maharajah who was in power for only a year or so. Ram Nath suspected that there was some truth in the ugly and persistent rumours, and on some nights this suspicion would terrorize him. Supposing someone should bring a case in the courts challenging his title! He would tell himself that the British Government had recognized his title by confirming him as the recipient of a land-tax grant collected from the estate in question. Nevertheless, the doubt would assail him.

His inner tranquillity thus disturbed, he would turn again to thoughts of finding some repose in love and song. He told himself that he had acquitted himself honourably as a householder: a husband, a father, and the head of an illustrious family. He now owed it to himself to discover his own talents for life. Also, he was curious to find out whether a special kind of depth was possible in the relationship between a man and a woman. With his wife, his relationship had been a very limited one. She bore and brought up the children. He became their father when they reached the age of about five or six. She ran the house to his entire satisfaction, and she was popular with all the relatives and with the poorer members of the community. So many members of the family had vixens for wives. He was thankful that he had been more fortunate, and he was even proud of his wife, whom he deeply respected.

At first he had hated himself for giving in to his desire for Ranu. But later, when he again wanted to visit Ranu, he realized that what he hated was that that old devil, as he always thought of Raja Muzaffar Khan, knew about his escapade and could not be trusted to hold his tongue. He might make a joke of Ram Nath even to the Dewan's son or to his other friends. Ram Nath felt that if only he could plan something for himself, secure from the knowledge of his friends, he would be liberated from the fear of exposure. He noted with satisfaction that the shops in Chandni Chawk were bringing in more rent than last year and that he would be able to finance his plan from this windfall. It was time to press ahead with his arrangements, decided the Dewan.

He had just reached this conclusion when, as he was returning one evening from his customary walk, he passed an emaciated dark man struggling under a sack full of pots and pans over one shoulder and a child on the other. Behind him walked a woman with an infant at her breast and, on her head, a battered string bedstead on which were laid other household goods. The man moved to the side of the road as the Dewan passed, and stood for a moment out of respect. Ram Nath looked closely at him and thought the man's face was familiar. He turned into his driveway. The heavy bloom of the evening was settling on the lawns and flower beds, and Ram Nath had the pleasant feeling of having returned to a familiar warmth. Was he escaping from something? He couldn't think, and yet a feeling of vulnerability remained. He was almost as afraid as in his earliest recollection of childhood, when he had thought he would not be able to control himself till he reached the bathroom.

For the first time that he could remember, there were no guests that night for dinner, and the large dining-room seemed to hide, in its unblinking vastness, some purpose that was alien to him. He felt the emptiness as an act of exclusion directed against him.

His own room was more kindly. But there was nevertheless a coldness in the way the things were arranged on his desk. They seemed to have a remoteness of their own. There was a certain orderliness about them which he did not share. He was there as someone who still had to find his place in life. He wondered what had happened. How had he fallen out of step? The more he tried to relax and tell himself that he was Ram Nath—Dewan, rich, powerful, respected—the quicker the pictures formed in his mind of all these landmarks, the less meaning they all seemed to have. He stroked his soft Pashmina jacket. It was there, but it had no relationship to him, there was no connection: the material might as well have been on the weaver's loom. He undressed and went to bed. He put an extra pillow under his neck and, propping himself in great comfort, opened Whitehead's *Adventures of Ideas*. The words conveyed little meaning—dry stuff, he thought. There was nothing there that he really wanted to know, and yet only yesterday this book had filled him with a zest for life and had seemed lucid and even beautiful. He put it down and sighed. He recollected some verses from the poets which dealt with the futility of life. In the past these couplets had always given him solace. If life was futile, then he was not responsible—someone else was, the creator was, and he could leave it all to him. But now the poets, too, seemed to know nothing about life. This cold, hard thing around him was assuredly real. This was some manifestation of life which he had been neglecting and which now was insisting on being recognized. It was a granite presence that he was unable to penetrate. He was like a fly on its surface.

He sighed again and turned out the light. If he could get rested, he would find himself in step again. But in the dark he was suddenly back again at the point of time that evening when, at the close of his walk, he had been suddenly confronted by the man and woman carrying all their possessions and their two children. He looked into the face of the man again. Yes, he knew the face! It was one of the sweepers living in his servants' quarters who was having to leave because the room was required for storing some pieces of derelict furniture which, for some reason, the Dewan's wife had decided to store instead of throwing away. The family occupying the room had begged to be allowed to stay on— they had even said that they would store the furniture in the room and use a corner of it, but that was not acceptable. Now they would have to find other lodgings and another job. Ram Nath tossed as he recollected all this. The man had looked miserably underfed, and though there was a chill in the autumn air, he had worn only a torn muslin shirt. His wife and children were no better clad, and yet there they were—going out into the world undoubtedly without enough money to buy themselves even two days' food. Would they have to starve now so that the broken pieces of furniture, which would never again be used, could be stored?

He told himself that he was being stupid. The man would probably find work the very next day and be as well off as he had been on the Dewan's estate. Ram Nath turned over, but his bed seemed even more uncomfortable on this side. He turned back to the other side and drew up one leg. That was better. He dozed. His leg felt heavy. He could hardly put it down. Funny, he thought. He had never known anything to be so heavy that it was difficult to put down again! He forced his leg down and tried to raise his other leg.

He awoke in a sweat, panting with the strain of the effort to raise his leg. In the split second between dozing and coming awake again, he was very confused. There were two overlapping images in his mind. He himself was the emaciated, hollow-chested sweeper with the heavy sack on his head; and he was also Dewan Ram Nath, walking home with the sweeper grovelling at his feet, gripping his leg and begging to be allowed to stay on in the out-house. He felt utterly exhausted. The dual image, now that he was awake and could analyse it, seemed to be the whole of life. It was a pincer movement: the sweeper on the one side and his own elegant loftiness on the other. He could break the pincer only by unhinging the point of coincidence of the two forces. Could he break the point hinging the fate of the sweeper and his own? He wanted to run into the streets to look for the sweeper and take him back. He wished he could give an immediate order that the furniture was to be thrown out at once and the room replastered for occupation by the displaced family. He jumped out of bed and rubbed his eyes. He went toward his clothes to change, and then asked himself what he was doing. There was a raw wind coming in through the open window which hit him in the pit of a very empty stomach. He felt weak and scraggy. He looked at his watch. It was three in the morning. He could not possibly go out to look for the other leg of the pincer, nor could he get the servants to clear the room.

He was very tired. He lay down again and turned out the light. Soon he was walking rapidly out of the house in his pyjamas. He felt ashamed of himself. His feet were bare and the cord of his pyjamas was rudely showing. He tucked it in and smiled to himself. It was extraordinary to be walking like this, but he was happy. He wondered what he was doing, and realized that he was carrying a large sack. He turned around. Behind him were the sweeper and his family, barely able to drag themselves along. He was no longer walking away from the house. They were all coming home and he was leading the little procession. What would the other servants say? he wondered. Say? They would say nothing; they would go and get the room ready for the returning family. But what would his wife say? . . . And he was awake again.

Ram Nath lay on his bed. He felt that he had entered a new door. There was much to be done in this room. The door had brought him out of doom, he felt. He had to do that which the door implied, otherwise he would return to the nightmare of the evening before. He had to follow through. He got out of bed and, pulling on a light Pashmina robe, he sat on a small carpet and meditated for a few minutes. Then he rose and walked straight to his wife's bedroom. She was not there, for it was already ten in the morning and she was with the cooks, giving them instructions for the day. He paced about the veranda at the back of the house, waiting for her to return.

"Rajeshwari Devi, please have that out-house emptied at once. We can sell the furniture, but we must have that sweeper back."

Rajeshwari looked up, wondering what he was talking about. Then she pieced it together. She rarely questioned him when he appeared to be determined. That happened infrequently, so that she had a large field left entirely to herself. She was not sure that he was determined on this issue.

"Dewan, why do you want the sweeper back? We don't really need him," she asked, using the formal style of address.

"But of course we need him. The drive looks unkempt, and look at all this filth lying about," he replied, waving his hand at the scraps of paper and other odds and ends on the pavement just outside the veranda.

But he had forgotten one point which his wife had not. "Shouldn't we wait till we know whether he is willing to return? I believe he had another job in view when he left. Do you know where he is?"

Ram Nath, in his anxiety to set right what had been done, had quite forgotten these matters. Supposing they failed to find the man; and, then, he might not wish to return where he had been turned out without any notice whatever. But the man must come back! He had an idea. "The other servants must know where he has gone. Tell one of them to go at once and fetch him back. We must have him back."

He went back to his room, called for his chauffeur, and gave him instructions to go immediately in the car and bid the man return. Gangu was surprised that he should be ordered to take the car for the mission, but he could see that the master was in earnest, and he set out at once.

Ram Nath felt better. He looked out of the open door to the close-cropped lawn, on which the last trace of dew made a gleaming patina. When it faded, the high sun would blink from the shorn stubs of grass. The woman he wanted was both the sun and the dew. She followed him, no matter what he did. This search for the sweeper was like the orderly shearing of the lawn, but the dew and the sun remained.

Funny. He was the most respectable of Brahmins, and the sweeper and the woman were whirling through his mind as if he were no more than one of those things set up at a fair for the pleasure of children. And all his reading pushed centrifugally away by this dominant whirligig. Was this what his life had come to? He looked out at the lawn again. No, the sweeper could not win this battle for him. Oh, yes! The sweeper must be taken in again, and with rejoicing. His wages would be modestly increased, and he would get Rajeshwari to give the man's wife and children a set each of new clothes—but the sun and dew were always there and he would have to come to terms with them. Supposing the sweeper were not to be found, or did not wish to return. The whirligig in his mind went faster and faster, desperately trying to keep his world in balance. With a great effort, Ram Nath dismissed the destructive thought. He felt calmer again. On the lawn, the dew had dried, and the sun sang out from the grass, drawing a hundred bees and wasps and tiny birds pecking away at the sweet stems sprouting toward the sun. In the distance he heard the regular click of the wheels of the Persian well, which was still used to draw water for the garden.

He went out into the garden. Two gardeners rose to greet him. He waved them back to their work and strolled past the borders of mixed flowers. The scent came up to him, hot and tight. It packed the air and rushed into him, so that he felt as if he were being drugged. He walked toward the eucalyptus trees and citadoras, whose slender white trunks and elegant, long, lacquered leaves always gave him a special feeling. And the water from the well, with its quiet, thin sparkle under the handsome trees, seemed to drain away the drugged feeling that the flower beds had given him. He looked across at the flowers. He wanted to return to them, but, instead, he stayed where he was and admired their loveliness and bravery. They had risen up high on their stalks, and in a matter of weeks they would wither and early one morning the gardeners would prepare the beds for the coming winter season. He told himself, with great determination, that all this was merely the world of matter and that there was no reason to be alarmed at these mutations of the season. He looked at the peepul trees and murmured a quotation from one of the poets:

> *"Clear, white bole of the peepul tree,*
> *Lacquered leaves, not too many, not too few:*
> *Lifting me to the top of its branches,*
> *Beseeching to be planted in my heart."*

Yes, yes, but why all this passage of life and then a new crop raised, as it were, on the death of that which had been there before? Supposing man did, after all, reach the moon. There, too, he would be the same withering creature. Look at himself. He had made life as pleasant as was possible. The house was filled with all manner of gadgets, and he had time to read and to speculate about the nature of things. And often this gave him satisfaction, but he understood so little about it all. He was kind to his family and, indeed, to all who met him. It was widely accepted that he was an honourable man and upright. It was true that one of his ancestors had procured a grant of land by practising some unseemly trick, but at least he himself deplored this occurrence, and it was no result of his efforts that the British had continued the grant to the family.

The chauffeur returned from his expedition and, immediately after garaging the car, came to the Dewan. He seemed uneasy, but tried to look as if nothing had happened. He had sensed that it was important to his master that the sweeper should return. Now he must act as if the whole thing was of no consequence whatever. He stood on one foot and picked up from the lawn a small piece of disfiguring paper which had escaped the attention of the gardeners. Then he cleared his throat and said:

"Sir, he does not come."

"But why doesn't he come, Gangu?"

"Maharaj, he must have been arranging to go for some time. He has another job. He was happy here, but his wife wants him to work in the other place. She has friends there," came the ingenious reply.

Ram Nath knew that this was not the truth. He turned away from his chauffeur and started to walk across the lawn. The bees seemed busier than before. They rushed at the dandelions and little flowering grasses and laid siege to the flower beds as though this conquest of sweetness was needed desperately if a crisis in the course of life was to be averted. Coursing up in him was the need to discover fully his own capacities for enjoyment and for the understanding of life. There was no use wondering about the wider questions unless he first got to know himself.

He walked back to the house. As he entered the hall, Rajeshwari came in from the back veranda. He knew that she would not humiliate him by talking about the out-house; but, somehow, he wanted to assert himself.

"Rajeshwari, do please sell that old furniture. It's nothing but junk. Why do we keep it?"

"Don't worry about these things. Since when did the menfolk of this household want to take upon themselves the work of the women?" came his wife's reply.

Ram Nath decided that it would not be wise to pursue the point with his wife. He grunted softly and walked quickly toward his study. There was something that he should not delay doing any longer.

CHAPTER TWENTY-TWO

ON HIS RELEASE from his second prison term, Jai spent more time at the village. Delhi seemed to lie prostrate after the heights to which it had risen in the great days of the political movement. Many of the old groups had been dissolved; Shabir had left on a trip to Europe; and when Jai looked up Dev Raj one day, he was poring over books of accounts and ledgers and, while he was still as unruffled as he had been in prison, now he had no time for conversation. So Jai was driven from Delhi.

In 1935, for the long summer vacation of the High Court,

Jai planned to go to the hills, but, en route, he stopped at Harbanspura. The monsoon was yet to break and the summer heat was at its fiercest, but there was no prostration at Harbanspura. On the day after his arrival at the village, Desa Singh and Pritam Singh called to see him.

"Come and join us, Jai Singh," said Desa. "We are meeting to talk things over."

Both Desa and Pritam looked brim-full of enthusiasm. Jai accompanied them to the big fig tree about a hundred yards south of the village. The dense shade of the great tree served as the meeting-place. Jhanda Singh, one of the oldest men in the village, was speaking in a tremulous voice to a group of farmers.

"In the old days, the rulers knew the meaning of government. When the number of farmers increased and there was no longer enough land in a village, the elders went to the Raja and told him of the situation. What did he do? Some of the men were offered service in the Raja's army or in the administration, and for the rest, new lands were found. Why, seven generations ago some of our own people from Harbanspura were given land north of Pathankot and that is how the village of Anandpura was settled. But now, what's to become of us and our sons and grandsons? What has happened to the art of government—that is what I would like to know."

He saw Jai in the crowd and, turning to him, he continued: "Jai Singh, you probably know the answer. You have read many books, and we hear that even the Big Governor of the English at Delhi is afraid of you. All I say is that the art of government must be learned again. If you ask me, I do not care who rules, but it must be rulership for the good of the people." And the old man mopped his face with the end of his turban.

"Bravo! Bravo, Babaji!" cried Desa. "The Government is useless, but we will show them. We will build our own school and sink our own electric well. Jai Singh is here now, and he will help us."

Immediately, plans were laid for a school and a well. Pledges were made of land, bricks, money, and labour. It was left to Jai to draw up the details and generally direct the project. The meeting broke up in an atmosphere of high hopes.

The next evening, as Jai was sitting in the open courtyard with his father, Prem Singh, Baba Jhanda Singh called from the outer gateway in his quavering voice:

"Prem Singh! Oh, Prem Singh! May an old man come in?" And before they could go to welcome him, they heard his shuffling steps on the high threshold of the door. Jai went to meet him.

Jhanda Singh's tremulous voice went on: "Son, that was a wonderful thing you did yesterday. The village is suddenly like a golden mustard field in the high spring, swaying under your spell."

Jai smiled at his romantic fervour. "But Babaji, I did nothing. It was you who inspired them and then they spoke up for the school and the well."

"None of that, Jai Singh! We must keep you close to the village. You come here so seldom. But I have a plan—" Jhanda Singh chuckled and shook his head several times. "Yes, I have a good plan. I must talk to your father."

Jhanda looked from father to son, and, putting down his big bamboo cane before perching himself on the charpoy, he said: "Well, Jai is not the old type of Rajput. If he were, how could I make this proposal? So let him stay with us, Prem Singh, and listen. Just as well he should."

They sat down, wondering what Jhanda Singh had in mind. The old man went directly to his point.

"Prem Singh, we must hold Jai close to Harbanspura. And we must do it with love. Don't you agree? If he were an orthodox Rajput, long ago he would have married a Rajput girl. Seeing he has not done so, I feel we should offer him the best that Harbanspura can give. Prem Singh, have you seen young Pritam's sister? She is more beautiful than Hir. She walks like a queen. Her eyes are like dark moths and her smile is like the new moon. Of course, she is a Jati, but then, Jai does not mind that. He must marry her. I have sounded Pritam Singh and he is thrilled at the idea—especially as that young devil Desa wants the girl. Tell me, isn't this a wonderful plan?"

Jai's face was full of amusement and he was about to jest with Jhanda Singh when he glanced at his father's face. The sadness that had come over it checked Jai's merriment. He knew the reasons for his father's sadness. Primarily, he was deeply full of anguish because he longed to see Jai married but knew he dared not even raise the matter with his independent son who had grown into a life so foreign to the established ways of the village. And he was dismayed that his son should be asked to consider marriage with a girl who was not a Rajputni.

Jai knew that Prem Singh would say nothing in reply to Jhanda Singh. And then Jhanda, too, would be sad and upset. So he struggled to reassure both the old men.

"Babaji, how kind you are to be so concerned for me. But you know I live in Delhi. I have to work there. And how

could a beautiful girl from Harbanspura live in the confinement of a city? She would pine away and die. Besides, I do
come often to Harbanspura now."

Jhanda Singh clutched Jai's arm. "Jai Singh, my son, you
are not wise in these matters. Just imagine even thinking that
the girl would pine for Harbanspura and die. Don't you
know, son, that when a girl loves a man, she doesn't die? She
lives for him!"

No, Jai did not know. It sounded so beautiful—"she lives
for him!" Would this beautiful village girl—he had never
seen her, but already her image had taken shape in his mind
—would she live for him in Delhi? A sense of limitless joy
in living suffused him. For a few moments he remained
dazed by the experience. Then he realized that again he
would have to break the deadlock of silence between the
two men without hurting either of them. He awoke to Jhanda
Singh's other world of dreams.

"Babaji, you know that tomorrow morning I am going to
Gurdaspur to give our applications for the school and the
well to the Commissioner. You see, we will need recognition
for the school and we will need the help of the Department
of Agriculture to get our well done quickly. I will set out
early, and tomorrow evening, when I return, I will tell the
village what has happened."

Jhanda Singh's old, bearded face lit up. He put his arm
around Jai. "That is wonderful, my son, wonderful. The
Guru will be with you, and you will tell us of your success
tomorrow."

Early next morning Jai set out. As a tactical move, he took
with him the village headman, who was an appointee of the
Commissioner. The Commissioner was an affable old Englishman who tried, very obviously, to conceal his chagrin at

having to receive Jai Singh—well known as a prominent worker for the termination of the order of which he himself was a symbol. Directing himself to the village headman, the Commissioner made a few perfunctory remarks about the prospects of the next harvest at Harbanspura. He did not even look at the applications and asked no questions about them. He then sent for one of his clerks and ordered him to "put up" the papers in due course. With that, he dismissed Jai and the headman.

At the village there was a sullen silence when Jai returned and related what had happened at Gurdaspur. Then the thunder began to roll.

"What sort of rulership is this?" demanded one of the elderly inhabitants.

"That's just it, brothers. That's why we agree with Jai that we must have other rulers—men like Gandhi, who know what is good for the people," said another of them.

Jai was deeply upset at the treatment they had received from the Commissioner. But underlying the disturbance within him was the realization that he had wanted to succeed brilliantly in order to justify Jhanda Singh's view that he deserved the beautiful sister of Pritam Singh. He wanted to tie himself to the village, to win his place in it by good deeds; then, perhaps, it would be quite natural that he should marry the beautiful girl.

Jai vowed that, without any delay, he would try again at Gurdaspur. The next morning he returned to the town. He went to see his friend Jagat Narain, the president of the District Lawyers Association. Jagat Narain was respected by the British officers for his legal skill, and often the Government had to engage him to strengthen the prosecution in its criminal cases. His natural gift for advocacy and his politeness

were invaluable assets in the law courts. Besides, there was
something very reassuring about Jagat Narain's large, heavy
figure in his long black coat. He wore a spotless white turban, under which his heavy-browed eyes sparkled kindly.

Jagat Narain laughed at his young friend, whose brilliance
and passionate devotion to the country he respected.

"So you are determined to have the New India begin at
your doorstep, Jai. Yes, why not? Like charity. . . . But you
want me to speak to the officers and jeopardize my whole
position? Don't you know that the police regard you as a
subversive character?" And he laughed again.

Jai smiled. "Yes, of course I am a subversive character,
from their point of view. But this time, from any point of
view, I am not being subversive. On the contrary, I am being
constructive—so the police should help me." And Jai flushed
at the thought of the beautiful girl in Harbanspura who was
the silent cause of his immediate return to Gurdaspur.

Jagat Narain took him by the arm. "Really, Jai Singh, you
would convince the Government that they should hand over
the country to you and your friends! Why don't you practise
seriously at the High Court and make money and a name
for yourself? But tell me now, what do you want me to do?"

"Very little, Jagat Narainji. I only want you to come with
me to the clerk of the District Commissioner and tell him to
read our petitions and quickly put them up to the Commissioner. That's all we want. We are convinced that if he
would but read our requests, he would give in to them."

"You know, I could call that sheer optimism and almost
moonshine if you have not, quite by accident, read the mind
of the Commissioner. He hates work and does what comes
easiest. If you have created even the semblance of a case in
your petitions, he will probably say: 'Let them have it, they

will soon find out these things don't help very much.' So you may be lucky. Come, let us go and talk to the clerk."

The clerk was very respectful when he saw Jagat Narain, who was one of the richest men in the town and its leading lawyer. He rose and saluted him very politely. Then he disappeared for a moment to tell one of the messengers to bring his callers a glass of fresh sugar-cane juice. As soon as Jagat Narain had explained the purpose of the visit, the clerk searched in a bundle of papers lying under his table. Taking some out, he read the applications. He seemed very puzzled. Jagat Narain, seeing this, suggested that he might ask any questions that occurred to him.

"There seems to be some error in one of the applications. It asks for an electric tube well. We have never heard of such a thing."

Jagat Narain explained that there was no mistake: what was asked for was the type of well which had been sunk two years earlier for the Gurdaspur water-works after the typhoid epidemic.

The clerk was now very pompous. "Then, how can a village be given what the District Headquarters received only two years ago?"

Jai wanted to tell him that it was high time the whole country had good water, but Jagat Narain had taken on the job as if it were a brief from one of his clients. He explained that a beginning had to be made some time, and that the well would give the people water for their fields also, so that it was not the same sort of case as the well for the town.

"Water for the fields! Jagat Narainji, we have no precedent for this kind of request. In any case, as it is for the fields, the views of the Agricultural Department must be obtained."

"That's reasonable enough," said Jai, remembering that the Agricultural Officer had helped in the matter of the plough cattle.

"And the other application must go first to the District Inspector of Schools," said the clerk, very pleased that Jai was going to raise no objection to his shuffling these papers off to someone else.

But Jagat Narain had something to say. "You are right, except that a school is not unprecedented. This is different from the case for the well. Why not put it up to the District Commissioner and let him see how much the village is going to contribute towards the cost of the school? When he sees that, he will tell the District Inspector to sanction the school quickly."

The clerk did not want to argue with Jagat Narain. It was said in the town that the longer anyone argued with him, the larger the number of points on which one would have to agree with him. So he undertook to put the school case up to the Commissioner. Thanking the clerk as they were leaving, Jagat Narain casually mentioned that he had an appointment with the Commissioner the next week and would ask him what he thought of the enterprising village of Harbanspura. It was certain now that the application for the school would be put up to the Commissioner.

When Jai returned home and the results of his efforts became known, the village was filled with enthusiasm again. Jai's own feelings were out of all proportion to the results he had achieved. He was elated because the villagers thought he was so much a part of themselves. Their evaluation brought him closer to the girl whom he now wanted to meet. He could not ask Pritam Singh to let him meet his sister. That would be much too direct. And undoubtedly Desa Singh, who was Pritam's neighbour, would learn of his request and then a really awkward situation would arise. There was no point in asking his own father to help, for Prem Singh would sigh deeply and beg him to name a Rajput girl. Jai decided to call on Jhanda Singh. He did so that very evening.

"Welcome. Welcome, Jai Singh," said the old man, clasping Jai to his bosom. But as Jhanda Singh embraced him fondly, Jai felt that some unexpected sorrow troubled the old man. They sat down on a hard wooden divan. Jhanda Singh was quiet—Jai had never before seen him in this mood.

His own impatience urged him on: "Babaji, the well and the school will soon be ours!"

"Yes, my son. I know, I know. And all your doing," answered the old man. But then he was silent again.

Jai simply had to be more direct. He went to the heart of the matter. "Then you no longer want me to be closely tied to Harbanspura? Tied with love?" he asked, smiling.

Jhanda Singh shook his head and sighed. "My son, I do want you to be tied to us. The Guru knows it." He stopped, as if waiting for the right words. Then, very slowly, he went on: "I went to Pritam Singh today. He told me that last night the girl was promised to Desa. That young devil has been insistent, and he has even bought another five acres of land to make it clear that he means well by the girl. So, that is an end of it for us, son." The old man clutched Jai's arm and sighed again.

Jhanda Singh's words seemed to turn the night into a great grey vacancy. Suddenly Jai felt terribly alone and weak. He moved his foot as if to try to feel his surroundings; but they had ceased to exist. He could not understand what had happened. It occurred to him that *he* was not really here; that he was non-existent in Harbanspura. He would have to leave the village at once.

CHAPTER TWENTY-THREE

FRISKING WINDS were pouring down from the mountains. It was the first sign that the arduous summer days would soon be over. Jai decided that he would pay a brief visit to his family home in the Chamba Hills—only about eighty miles away—before returning to Delhi. He was passionately attached to the hills, but he had hung back from visiting them ever since he had plunged into political work at Delhi. The hills were so beautiful, so special a part of his life that he had not wanted to take to them his tense and struggling self; secretly he had hoped that freedom would come soon and that he could then go to his beloved hills, watching their beauty with a new exhilaration. So he had waited. But now it seemed foolish to deny himself any longer.

Although he felt acutely the heavy sorrow of the fugitive,

the hills took hold of Jai almost as soon as he left Harban-spura. For many years he had not travelled this road, but now the very smells and the dark shades of the night came up to him like old familiar friends. As the bus sped toward the foothills, the scents became cool and penetrating and the air reached down, refreshing his heat-filled body. The earth seemed to grow more meaningful with its tone of heavy, dark foliage, and soon the hills crouched round like large, friendly animals.

The next day, at the bus terminal, Jai stepped into the middle of a gentle, eggshell-blue morning. Wanting to take in all this loveliness, he set out alone on the steep, strenuous, mile-and-a-half climb to the family house on the hilltop.

Sheru, the old caretaker, greeted him with a beaming face and a stream of lilting short sentences: "The forest is fine. Like a new bear pelt. But no fruit this year. Too much frost here. Good for the spring, though. What water in that spring of ours! You remember, Jai Singhji, what I told you. The old kings of Chamba drank this water. They weighed the water from all the springs in the land, and this weighed the least in one hundred and twenty-seven valleys."

Jai smiled as the familiar talk reverberated softly, and he asked: "How are all the people?"

"Oh, happy and unhappy. Blessings and troubles. Darau-padi, that beautiful devil, left Gangu." Gangu was his brother. "That was five years ago. Then she married at least four times, and God knows how many gutters she has slept in with whoever happened to be around. But no one keeps her now. She looks terrible—serves her right for leaving Gangu. Of course, he's a fool, too!"

For the next few days Jai spent all his time alone in the

hills. None of the houses in the neighbourhood was occupied. There were quiet and space. Yet, at first, to Jai the mountains looked shrunken and somewhat weary. The vast green slopes on which he had been lost in the mist in his childhood now yielded their entire mystery to fifty or sixty paces; and the valley to the cattle-pond where he had one day seen a panther drinking was only a dip in the hills.

But this readjustment of the proportions of his memories did not damage his feeling for the hills. They seemed, in fact, to come closer to him, to become even more intimately part of his life. They were no longer capricious and ominous, and the voice of the stream in the valley seemed sweeter and more immediate—like the singing of a maiden, a maiden who confused him at times.

Each day as the sun was about to set in the west over the foothills of Jammu, Jai climbed to the hilltop that overlooked the house and gazed across the ranges of lower hills and plateaus to the great plains of the Punjab, in which the curving rivers lay gleaming in the oblique rays of the sun. The land stretched on beyond the rivers to a hazy dimness that finally merged with the horizon. Nothing had ever moved him so deeply as this sight. It drew all of him to the sadness of the patiently waiting plains of India. At this hushed hour of evening the hills seemed to lift him up to their heights to give him back, renewed, to the land to which he belonged.

On the fifth day of his stay Jai was completing his walk around the four-mile road that girdled the hill. As he came round the last bend, he noticed two figures very slowly climbing the steep road below him. They broke their journey by stopping and resting every few minutes, and the contrast between his own strong stride and their halting progress impelled him to quicken his step still more—perhaps they were struggling against some infirmity and needed help.

He was but a few paces from them when they gained the flat surface of the road on which he was approaching. The couple stopped and panted for breath. Then the woman spoke and the man replied.

Her voice sounded musical but rather hard. "Papa, we've done it at last! And the breeze is wonderfully invigorating." It was unmistakably Geeta's voice.

And the reply, in a self-assured, heavy, flat tone, was that of her father, Pandit Brij Krishen, the great national leader. "One does everything, eventually. This air seems unpleasantly cold to me."

Just then they heard the crunch of Jai's sandals on the gravel surface of the road and both of them turned. Jai saw the haughty challenge of Brij Krishen's glance and a brittle, superficial recognition in Geeta's face. He raised his hands in salutation and stopped. He felt his lone communion with the hills cease with his last step forward. In the brittleness of Geeta's look there was another quality, which he could not immediately identify. She seemed to want something from him.

Geeta recalled to her father who it was that stood before them. Brij Krishen was appeased, and after a few remarks he invited Jai to visit them. As soon as it was decently possible, Jai fled to his house atop the hill. The next morning a young hill boy came with a note. They wanted him to lunch with them.

At lunch, Geeta said that she wished to explore the hills and that she knew Jai was familiar with every inch of the terrain. Perhaps, thought Jai, this was all she wanted from him. They arranged to set out on the following morning to explore the nearest hills. Jai enjoyed the dips into the valleys and the steep ascents. For the first two days Geeta laboured by his side. He thought that she was doing well and that, with practice, her hill legs would improve; but on the third day she struck, and every now and then she would implore him: "Wait! I can go no further. Let us rest awhile."

While they stopped to rest, she would probe him. She kept bringing the conversation round to Lena, but Jai had not seen her for years—not since the period before their first imprisonment. But his face reddened at the mention of her name, and Geeta was silent for a while, dismayed at this sign of continued emotional attachment to Lena.

The next day Geeta was charming and gay. She wanted Jai and was determined that he should respond to her. She realized, however, that she would have to change her role and act the unsophisticated girl. Again she climbed and ran gaily down the hills with him, and now, when she talked, Jai felt the hardness in her voice melting. He tried to read the look in her face—he could no longer see a claw in it as if she were going to tear something out of him. Time and again he searched her eyes. She was conscious of his gaze and let him look at her.

Jai's blush when she mentioned Lena had deepened Geeta's resolve to get even with the other girl. She remembered how Lena had quickly established herself with the young people to whom she had introduced her. She was determined to prove to herself that she, too, could easily succeed where Lena had.

To charm, gaiety, and simulated girlishness, Geeta now added a passionate interest in the Chamba Hills, for she realized how close to his heart Jai held them. She raved about

every hillside and every valley, heightening his zest to be
with her. He softened toward her and began to talk more
expansively. She was quick to follow up this evidence of his
increased interest, taking his arm whenever the path was
difficult and leaning on his shoulder at the end of a steep
climb.

Jai had started out on these daily excursions very gingerly,
with little predisposition toward the girl or her father, and
warned by the sharp claw he had at first detected in her
look. But after a few days of her fresh, unaffected charm
he felt that he was walking in another world. He had in-
tended to be in the hills only about ten days, but now de-
ferred his departure indefinitely.

Geeta was finding it difficult to adhere to her resolved
course. She had been watching intently Jai's growing submission, and had imagined herself a kind of pedestaled vic-
trix when the time of his surrender came. But now, when
she believed that she had him in her power, the change in
her own feelings surprised her. She had grown very fond of
him in the days they had spent together. In a sense she resented this new feeling and tried to fight it off, but inexora-
bly it took possession of some part of her which now tried
to ensnare the future.

"All this walking every day! I will never again want to be
carried round in a car!" she proclaimed as they sat down to
picnic in the Bathri valley.

"Oh, you'll be carried around in a car soon enough. The
hills are special. On the plains even walking is different," replied Jai.

"Perhaps what I will really miss will be the company," she
said a little more quietly.

"Does that mean you are not planning to be in Delhi next winter?" he asked, looking directly at her.

"I hadn't planned to." She stopped and drank some orange juice.

She did not quite clear the ambiguity, but later gave herself away.

"In Delhi you don't have any time for this sort of life, do you?" she asked.

"I haven't known this sort of life in Delhi," he answered.

The next day they planned to reach the top of Dain Kund, the hill of the dark spirits, the highest peak in the vicinity. They set out early and reached the top just before lunch. Geeta was really elated and felt that she had won her spurs as a "hill woman."

Jai twitted her: "The hill women here trudge forty miles a day and think nothing of it!"

After luncheon she laid her head in his lap. She looked up at him as if to say she was tired and needed him. She lay still for a few minutes. Then she put her arms around him and drew him down to her. Her heart was beating very fast, and the warmth of her body, heightened by the morning's climb, rose fiercely to him. She kissed his mouth passionately and held him close to her.

Thereafter their daily walks were directed to finding the secret nooks and the hidden arbours; and the hills richly rewarded their enterprise. No adept at these intimacies and restricted by deep inhibitions and nervousness, Jai at first held back. But soon he was caught up in the new rhythm and never had Geeta known a more ardent and ready lover.

The days passed swiftly by, all in a gentle September haze. Then Geeta had to leave. Her father was insistent and she could not oppose him. Jai visited them often in the last days of their stay, and Pandit Brij Krishen seemed to approve. As they were leaving, the Pandit took Jai warmly by the hand and said: "And thank you, Jai Singh, for having shown Geeta round these hills. She really knows them now, thanks to you. Come and see us when you can. Namaskar!"

The next day Jai also left, returning immediately to Delhi. The High Court had opened after the summer vacation and his clients were anxiously awaiting his return.

CHAPTER TWENTY-FOUR

WHEN Lena came home after her second term in jail, the sense of returning to life and wanting to hold fast to it was even stronger than it had been at the end of her first period of imprisonment.

She was pleased that her father pampered her. It softened the hard, accumulated frustrations and long deferments endured in jail. Pandit Dharma Das bought his daughter a car for herself, and it pleased her immensely to be able to come and go as she wished. She wanted to find two people: Prakash and Jai. She made contact with some of Geeta's friends whom she had met two years earlier. They were still a gay group, but none of them seemed interested in those of their companions who had left Delhi. It was not until her third meeting with them at Maiden's that she learned that Prakash's regiment was up on the northwestern frontier near Landikotal. The news was like an avalanche of sadness hitting her. She drove home, and for the next two days she was like a slack bow. She had no impulse to go out or even to walk in the garden.

Meanwhile, she learned that Jai was at his village, so that she had to allay the slight curiosity about him that still remained in her. After a few days she again drove around restlessly, but the obedient movement of the car remained just mechanical, producing no zest for life. She tried to find other interests, but it was no good. She struggled on for a few more days and then had to admit to herself that she was in complete despair.

In her wretchedness she went to her mother, now bedridden, and said that she wanted to meet people.

Shanti Devi opened her eyes wide as if to see the situation more clearly. "Yes, my child, of course you must meet people. But you do go out quite a lot?"

Lena shook her head. "No, I don't go out now—I don't know where to go." She sighed heavily and added, taking her mother's hand: "Mother—Mother, do you think you—you and Papa could arrange for me to meet someone I could marry?" She blushed and stopped.

Her mother looked alarmed. She had expected, or rather feared, that this was what might happen. She herself stood for the rights of women, including the right to choose a husband, and she had always assumed that it would all work out well for her own daughter; but at the back of her mind was also the fear that possibly it might not.

Now she could only splutter: "But—of course. Of course, we must. Your father has always wanted to do that for you."

Lena looked at her mother, her eyes brimming, but also in them was a sort of apologetic flicker directed toward Shanti Devi's known feminist convictions.

Later that evening Shanti Devi told her husband of Lena's request. The old man raised his face with a sanctimonious look. He did not criticize his wife. He could see that she was suffering under the weight of her responsibility for Lena's present state, and, besides, she was in precarious health. Dharma Das sighed and, passing both hands over his face, said: "This will need immediate attention and my best efforts. The girl is no longer young. Who will have her now?"

Shanti Devi said in a very tired voice: "Yes. But you will succeed. Lena is very beautiful."

Dharma Das was not so optimistic. "Beauty is not what gets a woman a good husband. But, thank God, she is well educated and she is quiet. And—oh, well, I shouldn't say this perhaps, but I am rich and her husband will be a very fortunate man. That helps, undoubtedly. Of course, I am not going to buy a husband for my daughter."

The next morning he put his arms around Lena and said to her very tenderly: "Don't worry, my child, don't worry. It will soon be all right." Then he set out to see some of his older friends and to consult them about likely young men.

After a month or so, Lena noticed that self-conscious-looking young men were beginning to arrive at the house to call on her father. Most of them never returned, but two of them were introduced to her: in itself a forward step in the strict convention of arranged marriages. But Lena did not find them in the least pleasing. On each of these occasions Dharma Das looked disappointed, but cheerfully he continued his search.

Meanwhile, Jai was in Delhi again and Lena met him at a meeting called by some of their old political associates. He was looking his best. The mountains had given his body a wiry litheness, and his closeness to Geeta had fired something throughout his being. He looked exceedingly well and tremendously alive. Lena was quite taken aback. She had not remembered that his personality was so powerful. But somehow it did not come near her. She admired him, but nothing drew her to him.

Jai, feeling the inner beat of life, at once realized that Lena was lacking something. She stood there, casting a sort of hollowness before her. There was no ambience, no light. He felt a sort of anguish on her account. He wanted to go up to her. But he could not: something held him back. He greeted her smilingly from across the room, but that was all.

Lena was pleased to see Jai, but she was relieved that she had not wanted to be close to him; then it seemed to her curious that this should be so. Before seeing him again, she had feared that there would be some sadness in their meeting and that she would perhaps regret their having grown apart. But now as she went around and met people, a strength seemed to rise in her which sloughed away her feeling of despair. A husband had not yet been found for her, but she no longer felt lost.

Two days later there was a phone call for her. It was Prakash. He was on leave from his regiment, and he asked if he might come and call on her and her parents. He still sounded manly and direct, just as she had known him; and his question was as if they were taking up the conversation from where they had left off over two years before. She was delighted at the sense of continuity this gave her. Without asking her parents, she said he should come.

She told Dharma Das and Shanti Devi that a Captain Prakash was coming to see her. They both looked at her with parental willingness to wait and see. Soon Prakash drove in. He was dressed in uniform—a barathea suit, a peaked cap—and he now wore the insignia of a major.

The servants gazed at this strange person. It was the first time that an Indian army officer had come to the house. In the old days most of the visitors had been political workers, and recently relatives and friends of Pandit Dharma Das had predominated.

Prakash climbed the marble steps to the veranda two at a time. He saw Lena come through the hall door. Her face flushed a little and her dark eyes lit up. She felt something rise in her so thickly that when she first opened her lips to greet him, no words came. She coughed to release the tension and then weakly said: "Hello." Prakash stopped and saluted very smartly. His squarish face was bronzed by outdoor activity. His eyes were clear and friendly, and his full, kindly mouth seemed to express a constant readiness to say and do what was required of him. As his hand came smartly down from the salute, Lena saw the firm quiver of his muscular body, and that, too, reassured her.

Prakash thought that she looked even more beautiful than the last time he had seen her. Her face was a little thinner, which gave it more form, and her eyes were more alive, more unashamed in their expression.

He said to her: "Lena, you are just as I have always thought of you, only more so, if you know what I mean."

She smiled and said: "It is so good you are here."

She led him to the drawing-room. He saluted both her parents, and in the good form of the Punjab he went up to her father and lowered his hand toward his feet for a moment. He asked after their health, and soon he was saying that they should spend some time at his village and benefit from the fresh country air. Lena and he would ride out on his estate and look at the men at work. He was unaffectedly warm and friendly. It was as though what he knew of life was a gift that he felt he had to share with them. Dharma Das at once melted, and Shanti Devi had already made up her mind to be on his side.

The next morning he came to see Pandit Dharma Das and asked if he might marry Lena. Dharma Das approached the question of Prakash's family. He learned that Prakash was a rich landowner. But, although he came of the proud Jat clan of the Punjab, he was not a Brahmin. How could Dharma Das make this acceptable to the family priests? Strictly, there could be no sacrament of marriage between a Brahmin and the other castes. Dharma Das's legal mind worked rapidly on the problem. No, it just would not come out right—unless, of course, they went through the absurd procedure of a civil marriage, which meant that they would have to renounce their religion publicly. Dharma Das said that he would have to take advice on this point.

Prakash understood the old man, and was not at all put out. Smiling, he said: "Very well, sir. I will call again tomorrow."

Dharma Das had his chauffeur drive him to Dewan House

immediately. Not that he thought anything of Ram Nath's ability, but he felt that the Dewan was a man of the world and might know the answer to their problem.

Ram Nath asked some details about Prakash and at once identified the family. "Oh, yes. A grandson of Kunwar Mangal Datta. A very fine family, very fine. You could do worse, Dharma Das."

"Yes. But you know he's a Jat. How shall we get the marriage performed?" asked Dharma Das, his face puffed out with serious, heavy thought.

Ram Nath jerked his face toward Dharma Das and widened his eyes. *"Hein?"* he asked impatiently, adding with a flourish of his hand: "That's easy. Easy, Dharma Das. My Pandits will marry anyone I tell them to. After all, these Jats are very respectable people. For all we know, they are Rajputs, and who wouldn't marry a Rajput these days? You just leave it to me. I'll settle that." And Ram Nath nodded his head quickly two or three times in Dharma Das's face as if to dispel his lingering doubts.

Dharma Das sat stolidly for a few moments, but decided that he might as well accept Ram Nath's view. It seemed intrinsically right. The young man was rich, respectable, he had a big stake in the land, and he was a fairly senior army officer. It could not be illegal for anyone's daughter to marry a man with all that. It would just have to work out the way the Dewan said.

So it was all arranged. Early in 1937 the wedding took place. Prakash's people and friends came in a special train from Ambala, which was near his village. The Jat guests were a bit too lively for the Brahmins of Delhi, but the townspeople kept up their end by brilliant sophistication, which bewildered their rustic in-laws. There were two days of buntings, feasting, music, dancing, and illuminations. Lena's excitement was so great that she was only vaguely aware of the surfeit. Then with Prakash she went away to the beautiful Himalayan valley of Kulu, where they spent ten days before going on to his new station, Meerut, where the 16th Cavalry was now posted.

CHAPTER TWENTY-FIVE

RAM NATH had no desire to extend his material interests. There was no need to do so. He now had a mistress and found that it was not, after all, a very expensive business. He had often heard it said that a woman of that kind was never content with what she was given and bestowed her favours in proportion to the amount she was paid. But Ram Nath got all he wanted for a modest monthly allowance. Chambeli always contrived deftly to discover the mood in which he had come to her, and then she set out to invigorate, or calm, or amuse him as she thought he most wanted. Sometimes he would tell her of his business difficulties, and then she would always say something that helped or soothed him.

To him, she seemed the most normal person he had ever met, and though her career must often have been a difficult one, she was more truly contented than most people who talked loudly of the virtue of accepting one's lot in life.

Ram Nath now got more enjoyment than ever out of his scientific reading, and felt that he had devised a life ideally balanced among the things of mind, body, and spirit. For him, only a few years of life remained and he was thoroughly enjoying himself. He appreciated his wife more than ever before, and he even found it possible to be tolerant of his son, Dina Nath.

But this quietly balanced tenor of existence had to bow to the new forces in the country. So far, Ram Nath had been content to turn some of his money into city properties, but much of it remained in loose cash, and when there seemed more of that than was safe, gold was bought. Now his friends and relatives started making calculations of how much more he would have if he were only to invest his money in the timber business or in a colliery, or in one of the numerous industrial ventures in the country. In ten years—no, even in five years—if he was lucky, he would double his money. Besides, how was the country to develop unless those who had money put it to constructive use of this kind?

Ram Nath was persuaded, and he bought a colliery in Bihar. He also invested a large sum of money which was not required for any other purpose, in various Tata enterprises. All went as he had been promised. He was now earning vast sums of money, and when Geeta, his favourite niece, reached Delhi after her visit to the hills and a short stay at Lucknow with her father, he was on the point of setting up a soap factory. He had come to the conclusion that if India was to take her rightful place in the forefront of the nations of the modern world, more soap must be used in the country. He would, therefore, be contributing toward India's march to modern greatness in the new scientific age by increasing the production of soap. With great pride he told everyone of his scheme, and, being rich and old, he was listened to with great respect and everyone congratulated him on his enlightened public conscience. He felt better than ever, and threw all his energies into the planning of the factory. The figures showed that, once the factory went into full production, each year he would be earning a return of forty-three per cent on his money. Of course, he would have to pay tax on this income, but, even so, his net return would be very high, and this worried him. He decided to lower the price of the soap, but his advisers told him that if he did so, only the wholesalers and retailers would profit, without any advantage reaching the consumer. Some other way of easing his conscience would have to be found.

He greeted Geeta warmly. "Welcome, my dear girl! You are getting so fond of the sophisticated life of other parts of India that you are forgetting us altogether. But I must say whatever you are doing suits you. You are more beautiful than ever—and you always were the most beautiful girl in the country." And the old man embraced the radiant young woman.

He then told her of his new project, and how it had been devised to meet the needs of the people, and how he was being frustrated by the middlemen, who would make large profits and sell the soap no cheaper than the other brands. What was he to do?

"Uncle, people must have money to buy your soap. Will your workers be able to buy it?"

He thought a moment and then said: "Well, yes—I suppose they will be able to buy a little, buy not very much," wondering what would come next.

"Then, Uncle, you can let all the workers buy enough soap for themselves and their families at the price you will get from the wholesalers. This will not reduce your profits. You will still have your huge returns. And, secondly, why don't you either build houses for the workers or give them money on certain terms to help them build their own homes? You could even lend them part of the money, and you could get an architect to make a few designs of good, inexpensive houses. Oh, Uncle! There are hundreds of things you could do—and, please, do most of them."

"Why was I not told these things before, by my advisers? Of course these are the things to do. Do you know, Geeta, my child, everyone who has been advising me assumes that the workers must be treated like dirt. They never say so, but that is the assumption. I won't stand for it! But just think. If it had not been for you, I would have done exactly as the others. And I would have become like Ram Labhaya, the old devil, who always manages to look as though he were sitting on the poverty of his wretched workers," and the old man's face was red with disgust at the thought.

He continued, with his eyes fixed on Geeta: "Look at this girl! She has saved me from an evil fate which no one else was intelligent enough to discern. Really, what a world this is!"

Geeta blushed. Just then a servant came in and said that Jai Singh had asked to be announced.

The Dewan stopped. Noticing the colour rising in Geeta's face, he said: "Jai Singh? Who is this Jai Singh?"

Geeta tried to look composed, but she was aware of having

flushed, and in rather a fluster, she said very quietly: "You remember him, Uncle. He has been here many times."

Ram Nath looked puzzled and then blurted out: "Yes, yes, of course. The son of Prem Singh. Well, shall we let him come in?"

Geeta nodded, and Ram Nath signified his assent to the servant.

When Jai Singh entered, Ram Nath noticed that the brightness of Geeta's face was even further heightened. So that was what was happening, immediately concluded the old man. But he soon forgot about the matter: his mind was still on his soap factory.

Now that Jai Singh was there, and his own son, Dina Nath, who had come in with his wife, the Dewan felt it was his duty to tell them of his plans. He repeated the story of the project and included Geeta among his audience, forgetting that he had already told her. This time he elaborated the plans for special sales of soap to the workers, housing for them—all as part of his own ideas.

Geeta complimented him again and Jai agreed with her. But the Dewan's son, Dina Nath, adopted an injured expression and, in a grumbling voice, said: "Why should the effort to improve the world fall to us? It will only mean that we will earn less money than other people."

Ram Nath turned to his son. "On what basis do you make out that you will be earning the money that will come to us from the soap which will be made in our factory? I am not of that impression at all. All we are concerned with is the making of soap—and let us try to make it well. Perhaps we are entitled to a rental for the machinery and for the buildings, but must we rack-rent? Have we not just reduced rents on our estates, and do we not remit rents when conditions are difficult? Well, I am going to do the same sort of thing here, and more so because I do not want to make the mistakes my forefathers made on their estates."

Dina Nath was not sure he had followed all this, but he thought it wisest to say no more. A few minutes later he and his wife got up and excused themselves. When they had left, Ram Nath felt for the first time in his life that Geeta did not want his company. Had anyone else been concerned, the Dewan would have expected someone other than himself to withdraw, but with Geeta he was indulgent. He got up meekly and said that he had work to do in his office. He shuffled out of the room after giving Jai Singh a cold, hard look.

Geeta was still passionately enamoured of Jai. She had missed him terribly during the month or so which had elapsed since they were together in the hills. The real purpose of her visit to Delhi was to be with him. Jai had brought away from the time spent with Geeta in the hills a singing satisfaction that remained with him constantly. He had thrown himself into his legal work at Delhi, but, no matter what the pressures, the tediousness, the unreasonable demands of his clients, there remained a sweetness that would make him break into a smile at the most unexpected moments.

In Geeta's presence, now, he felt an intensification of that sweetness. She came up to him and held his arm hard as she searched his face with her eyes. Seeing the answering fire in them, she said: "Let me come with you now, to your rooms. Yes? Let me!"

He was taken aback at her suggestion, but as he felt her warmth against him, his first shock subsided. He pressed her to him and smiled assent. A few minutes later he left alone, leaving Geeta to follow.

They were together the whole evening. Geeta lost all count of time, and when Jai asked her whether she should not go back to Dewan House, she would not leave his arms. Very late that night they fell asleep. The dawn was just breaking when Geeta awoke, and then she vaguely realized the consequences of her action. There would be consternation at Dewan House over her disappearance for the night. She woke Jai. Hastily they dressed and he walked down with her. Near Kashmiri Gate, they came upon a wretchedly tired coachman in a tonga. They got in and jogged very slowly to Dewan House. Jai left her at the gate.

Geeta walked quickly up the driveway, hoping that she could slip into her room and that there would be no questions. But when the house came in view, she saw the figure of Ram Nath huddled in a large chair on the veranda. As she approached, he recognized her and Geeta could see the pieces of his distraught face coming together. He pushed his legs out from the large, tightly wrapped Kashmiri shawl and rose to meet her. His face was gaping now with a sad, questioning look. Geeta ran up and embraced him.

He murmured: "My darling child, my darling child. What happened?"

She shook her head. "I will tell you, Uncle. I will tell you everything."

That was enough for him. He did not press her, but his practical mind was working on what must immediately be done.

"I will ring the police myself." Then he looked at her. "I will just say it was all a mistake. It was a mistake. I went into my library and found you had fallen asleep reading a book. . . . That's best. They have no business to know about our private lives."

He called the police station and told them his story. Then he smiled. He had saved the honour of the family.

Turning to Geeta, he said: "Poor dear one. Go off to bed. We will talk later."

In her room, Geeta heaved a sigh of relief. The old man had been splendid. What would she tell him? She realized that it would be difficult to deceive him, for he had noticed something the previous day when Jai had called. Then she thought it out. What if she told him the truth? She could trust him: of that she was sure. But could she face him? Yes, she decided. She would have to tell him.

Later that day, in his study, she told him. Ram Nath felt that he should know what this really meant. Did she feel very much drawn to Jai? Geeta told him that she felt completely held by Jai as a lover. More than that she had not thought of. Rather nonchalantly she said: "Do you think I should marry him, Uncle?"

"Marry him? How can you think of it! Of course you should not," Ram Nath replied emphatically.

Surprised at his reply, she asked: "But why not?"

Ram Nath again answered immediately. "Because he is not a Brahmin."

Now Geeta was really curious. "But, Uncle, you supported Lena's marriage with Prakash, who was a Jat. Jai Singh is a Rajput."

"My dear child, that was different. Don't think I am being inconsistent. In both cases my advice is correct, and therefore it really is consistent."

Baffled, Geeta said: "But do explain, Uncle. I don't see it."

"My dear, of course Jai is a Rajput, and I know his father has a small piece of land. But, you see, all the Brahmins would object. He would not bring us anything. With Prakash it was different. He is very rich, and he brings all that to the Brahmins, and we Brahmins are used to receiving things from the people. In your case, we should just be giving you away. It's impossible!"

Geeta did not argue the matter further. She had not really thought of marriage.

Although she was more discreet, she saw Jai now almost every day and her time with him became a deep necessity, a habit of her life.

Jai felt very tender toward this passionate girl whose fire seemed so completely given over to him. Her presence filled his room and overflowed into his work and into every moment of his life. He had not asked her to marry him, but that, he felt, would certainly come and he wanted it to come from them both: that was how he reckoned it should be. There were days when she clung to him so much that she kept him from his work; but, thought Jai, once they were married, she would feel secure about him and would accept his need to work. However, as the days passed, more often than not Geeta would want him to give her all his time.

During this period Dewan Ram Nath grew to be very fond of Jai. At least three times a week he insisted on having him at Dewan House. The Dewan discussed all the details of his soap-factory project with Jai and came to accept the young man's advice on all matters concerning the factory. He appointed Jai his legal counsel for the project, and said to Geeta:

"That is a very fine man. Good brain and a good heart. If only I had had a son like that!" The old man sighed and shook his head.

On another occasion he said to Geeta: "I don't know what I would do without your Jai Singh. I am very fond of the man."

Geeta wondered whether he was going to change his advice about marriage between them, but the Dewan never mentioned the subject again. Perhaps, she thought, he wanted his earlier words to be forgotten and his real desire to be learned by implication.

For five weeks Geeta's and Jai's life together deepened. Geeta gave no thought to where it was leading her until suddenly one morning she did not feel the urgency to go to Jai's little apartment. Rather reluctantly she went; and on her return that evening she felt an ease and pleasantness at Dewan House which she wanted to keep. The next day she spent the morning talking happily with Ram Nath, and when evening came she could not bring herself to visit Jai, but sent him a note that she was unwell. On the following evening she was with him a little while, but she felt herself a stranger. It was as if she had decided something. The next morning she took a train to Lucknow. From there, Jai had a telegram: "MY FATHER NEEDED ME AT HOME URGENTLY. AM HERE TILL I DON'T KNOW WHEN. LOVE, GEETA"

Jai was stunned. He had noticed Geeta's restlessness for some days. He had wondered what had happened, but had never had the courage to ask her. Now he knew that he had feared her feelings might be changing. Wildly he hoped—maybe her father *had* needed her, maybe that *was* it.

CHAPTER TWENTY-SIX

JAI WROTE to Geeta, but rather impersonally. He hoped her father was better—he assumed she had had to leave suddenly because he had been unwell. He said perhaps she would return soon to Delhi. There was no reply.

For many days there remained in Jai's apartment an irradiation of Geeta's presence. He would wake in the morning and in the new light of dawn he could still almost see her everywhere in the room. It was only when he got up and, stretching himself, went to the big bay window which looked out on the gnarled peepul trees and at the busy life around Kashmiri Gate that there was a break from the pervading presence of Geeta. All the outside world seemed unconcerned. The trees always lured him away from himself. They were so alive and at the same time so calm. During the day they were still, and then in the evening the leaves would tinkle a little in the breeze.

Jai wished he could arrange his life simply, rather like that.

He tried to analyse how he had let himself be drawn into a relationship with Geeta. He had not been seeking anything, and yet his feeling for Geeta had become so much a part of him. How could it be that, without his volition, he had been taken so far along that now, cut off from Geeta, it was as though he lived in a half-world. He tried to shake himself free of the thing that held him, but it was intangible and still seemed to be outside the range of his volition. At times he would be saying something and the words would stop coming in the middle of the sentence, as though his thought had ceased to have any meaning or purpose.

He continued to see a good deal of Ram Nath. The old man had grown to trust him and they talked freely about everything: but Geeta was never mentioned. Then, one day Ram Nath said:

"Some people are like an April shower. They come with great intensity and then it is all over. There is nothing to be done about it even if it hurts."

As time went by, the hurt in Jai became deeper. His analysing had diverted his mind for a while, but because it did not explain anything, he let it cease and then he was confronted again with the bare fact of his dependence on love and affection and the great void created by their withdrawal.

He began to devote more time to conducting political meetings, and he started writing a history of the 1930-1 phase of the national movement. His mind was very keen. He read at an amazing rate, and facts and ideas seemed to weave themselves into a closely knit whole. It was as though all this mental activity were trying to fill the vacuum in him. He wrote faster and faster, but the emptiness was an endless maw.

Scores of letters came to him from the village asking him

to come and see how his efforts for the school and the well had borne fruit. He had put up a quarter of the money for the well and had sent a reliable firm from Bombay to the village to do the drilling and install the diesel engine. As his life at Delhi had become purposeless, at Christmas he went back to Harbanspura for the High Court vacation.

It was bitterly cold as the train approached Gurdaspur. Two of the young men from the village had come to the station, bringing a spare mount for Jai. In the cold morning air they galloped into Harbanspura. The villagers put on a celebration for Jai. There was a leafy archway in front of his ancestral home, and the village musicians were playing romantic airs.

Desa Singh has insisted that his wife—he had married the beautiful sister of Pritam Singh—should also turn out to greet Jai. Desa put a heavy garland of marigold around Jai's neck and proudly presented his wife. He whispered to Jai: "Jai Singh, she is lovelier than roses. Brother, it is a rainbow all the time!"

Jai greeted the lovely girl. She stood beside Desa Singh, beautifully formed, and smiling. The image of Geeta filled Jai's mind. He quickly looked away and, turning to all of them, he called: "And the well—it goes?"

A chorus came back: "Goes and goes, Jai Singh. Don't you see the whole land green with the sprouting wheat stalks? Come and see!" And they led him to the well.

The engine was chugging away and the water poured out, a steady silver stream. On a stone over the waterspout were written words from one of the Upanishads:

When thou pourest upon them,
Then these creatures of Thine, O Life,

Are filled with bliss, knowing
There will be food for all their desires.

Jai divided the week between chatting with the men at the village and taking lonely rambles in the wide, open country-side. Physically he was exhilarated; and the great expanse of country on three sides and, in the distance to the northeast, the outline of the Himalayan hills gave him a sense of all-embracing perspective. But this did not extinguish the hurt caused by his experience with Geeta. On the contrary, he came now to regard the hurt as part of his inmost self, as part of the process of life. It remained in him as did his political convictions, his work, his deep feeling of joy at the sight of the mountains, and his interest in law and writing. He no longer tried to escape from it or to find a state of be-ing which would exclude it.

When he stopped struggling against the pain, a great ten-sion within him subsided. Now he knew that, driving him-self very hard in his work and in the Movement, he had skimmed the wide surface of life. He had failed with both Geeta and Lena because he had not really been open to the experience of deep affection. In the midst of his hard gallop and his headlong, single-minded devotion to the Movement or to whatever other work he was doing, he had, as it were, bent over to the side a little to maintain some contact with those whom he had wanted to love. He had attempted the impossible, but could he give up his work? No, that could never be, and now he realized that just as he was work- and freedom-absorbed, he would also have to be love- or friendship-absorbed if he was ever to taste the fulness of close relationships with people.

His musing went on. He realized that here at Harbanspura, too, he had long ago lost the deep thread of life. He had worked hard with the men for the well and the school, and that was good. But for Desa Singh, Pritam Singh, and even for the older people—his old father, Prem Singh, and Kharak Singh, the village headman—and for their women-folk, the school and the water from the well had already become no more than little flowers blossoming from the deeply rooted life they lived.

As he was returning from his evening ramble that day, he felt painfully excluded from the life of the village. He was passing Desa Singh's house. The main door of the front courtyard stood wide open, and within, on the right, a fire glowed over the open oven, from which the hot, rich smell of freshly baked bread was rising into the evening air, together with the sweet pungency from the green hay at which the cattle were chewing on the opposite side of the courtyard.

Jai stopped, and heard the sound of laughter and merriment coming from a room to the right of the courtyard. Then Desa's wife came tripping out to the oven, took two freshly baked unleavened chapatis, and ran back to the room.

Jai felt acutely the outsider he had made himself and decided not to enter the open doorway. He was an alien and would spoil their mirthful happiness. Perhaps he was not even an alien, for he knew they would accept him, but it was his nothingness that would negate their happiness. If he went into Desa's house, he would add no warmth. He had nothing to give. Sadly he walked to his own home.

The next day he set out for Delhi. He knew that a great deal of activity awaited him, and he knew also that what he had been learning about himself did not mean that he was to shrink from his work. The war that had broken out in Europe in the previous September was now beginning to affect the lives of the people. Foreseeing a long struggle ahead of them, the British had started a recruiting drive in the country. With a potential manpower of over fifty millions and with a stagnant economy in which there were many millions of unemployed, it was not difficult to find recruits. In addition, there was now a certain degree of bewilderment about the matter. The people felt that they should acquire the various skills and experience which an independent country would need. They believed that the creaking Imperial façade would crumble at any moment now and that they would then have to take control themselves. To Jai, this was indeed a dilemma: he himself did not intend to enlist, but he was constantly being asked for advice by young men around him. He was against help for the British, and most of all he disliked aiding their armies, but there was also his conviction against Fascism and tyranny in any form and his appreciation of the argument that, whether he liked it or not, here was an opportunity for training many young men in the country. He felt that those concerned should consider all these aspects and make their own decision.

Another matter that took his time was Dewan Ram Nath's insistence on seeing him every day. He generally lunched at Dewan House. Ram Nath was still very alert. Some days he would reminisce, and then he would usually end up by telling those present how fortunate they were to be growing up in a country that was rubbing its eyes and emerging from a long slumber. On other days he would warn them not to forget their traditions and the depth of life which had been fashioned through thousands of years of experience in the country. On yet other days he would inveigh against the Congress Party, against the British, against the moneyed classes, against the Brahmins, against the sectional leaders who imagined that they would gain by dividing the country—against almost everything. On these occasions he would turn to Jai:

"Don't you think I am right, Jai Singh? Now, tell me."

Jai would tactfully but very deftly point out other considerations so that finally it became clear to the Dewan that he had been taking an extreme position. Then the old man would grunt and, twirling his silvery moustache, say:

"Hm-m—well, that's true, that's true. You see, things are not so bad after all. I thought as much! We will get along somehow, my friends."

One day after lunch, just before Jai left, Ram Nath took him aside and said: "You know that little devil Geeta has been in Calcutta for six months. Never even told me. I believe she's having a rather gay time. Well, what can you do with young people!"

CHAPTER TWENTY-SEVEN

ALL Ram Nath's business and property interests were doing
excellently. Prices were beginning to rise, and money was
pouring in from rents and dividends and from his mills. Besides, the whole output of the new soap factory had been
bought by the Government for the armed forces at a good
price. There was no expenditure for advertising, agencies,
commission, and none of the bother of these things. He had
insisted, however, on holding back a small percentage of the
soap produced, and this went, as he had planned, to the
workers at cost price. Ram Nath was determined not to let
this glut of money blunt the fine edge of his spirit. He decided that he must think of improvements that might be introduced on his estates and in his factories.

He would start with an experiment. His old friend Raja
Muzaffar Khan had died in the winter of 1940, and the
Adampur estate was for sale. Ram Nath decided to buy the
estate and install electricity, which would be extended to

the houses of the tenants at the orchard and to the farms on the outskirts of the estate. Also, he would put in modern plumbing and sanitation so that the house could be really comfortable. He could then move into it part of his library, making Adampur a quiet and scholarly sanctuary from the rush of Delhi.

The estate was bought, and all the planned improvements were carried into effect. With high hopes, Ram Nath went out to the estate for a week-end, but he found it terrifyingly lonely. He could neither work nor rest in such complete isolation. Besides, there was something rich and sensuous about the estate which defied the mechanical touch of electricity and the new sewage system. It was not just loneliness that he felt. It was a sensual longing that kept uprooting him from whatever he tried to do. He sighed to himself. The experiment was clearly incomplete; something would have to be added. He stopped short. He knew that he was leading to just one conclusion—but he felt that he had to argue with himself, for if there was just the one possible conclusion, why had he not expressed it long before? He told himself that it would be too risky to install his mistress here. Tucked away where she was, in the middle of the old city of Delhi where many people lived their own lives, he had been able to keep his relationship with her a secret from everyone of social consequence. But once she was brought to Adampur, some friend or other paying him a visit would see her or hear about her from one of the neighbouring peasants and then what would the world think of him? They would laugh at him—a man of over seventy keeping a young mistress.

But these arguments were of no avail. In truth, Ram Nath had such vivid recollections of the warm lechery that he had indulged in at Adampur in the company of his late friend, the Raja, that as soon as the property had been put up for sale he had wanted it because it would perpetuate for him, in these last years of his life, the pleasant taste of his association with the place and also give him the hope of fresh experiences of the same kind. If he had not formulated all this clearly to himself, it had been because of the fears with which he was now struggling.

He was in urgent need of someone who would help him lift this weight of unfulfilled sensuousness at Adampur. He decided to send for his present mistress at once. The car went, with his chauffeur, Gangu, and brought back the desired treasure in the dead of night. Immediately she comforted the poor old Dewan, and then, the next day, her minstrels also arrived. In the evening there was singing and dancing, and the Dewan was content except for one gnawing discomfort. He wanted someone to whom he could explain all this —someone who would be intelligent and sympathetic; who would perhaps join in the revelry and realize how important it was as a means of using to the fullest degree the faculties with which one was endowed, but for which the normal social outlets did not provide. As an enlightened, intelligent man, he felt it was a pity that he should not be able to explain to someone that there was nothing wrong in what he was doing and that the secrecy was not of his choosing but merely a concession he made to society.

Of course, he had in mind a person from his own social class with whom he could converse freely. But he could think of no one who would be just right for this very intimate association. So he compromised by introducing Gangu to partnership in his revelries. Gangu, too, was a Brahmin, and not entirely unlettered. Ram Nath found him much more intelligent than he had imagined, and deeply sensitive to poetry and song. It was an ideal partnership for the Dewan, who was always able to have the lion's share of everything for himself.

Thus did Ram Nath enjoy the fruits of his prosperity. It was his practice to go out to Adampur each Friday at about noon. There he would eat a meal prepared in the classic Moghul manner, with at least eight dishes of meat, rare-scented saffron rice, and the most exquisitely balanced condiments. He would eat alone, with some of his retainers standing in the background, the chauffeur occasionally appearing in front of the table, and his new mistress, Zohra, sitting by his side but not eating. He talked as he ate—at random, about the estate, improvements yet to be made, the surrounding agricultural land and the yields of the last harvest, about a new poet of whom he had heard, and about some poet of the classical days who resembled the new star but had written with equal grace and facility in Persian and in Hindi. When he finished, he would lie down to take his siesta, but always, on Friday, he was hungry for the caresses of Zohra. After a few minutes of tossing on his bed, he would send for her and ask her to put her hands on his head. She would take his head on her lap and stroke his hair, massaging the back of his neck and the lobes of his ears. Then his whole body would cry out to be comforted, and in the afternoon she would lift him into a swoon of ecstasy. At about four Zohra would leave him to rest, and he would lie still, feeling the cold, wet perspiration under his beard on the tender skin of his throat. It would be like an anointing that had been left on him in some deeply climacteric ceremony, and now he was left to himself to recollect its meaning and to transmute the experience into the speculative terms that his mind sought.

This was peace. No, it was more than peace. It was life meeting life at the core of being and yet retaining its individuality. It was the rhythm of the dualistic and the monistic, of the creation, and of nirvana. He would rest till he was awakened at sunset by the cawing and singing of the thousands of crows and other birds returning to roost in the orchard for the night. The clamour of the birds always pierced him as a sort of death-call swallowed up by the night—so much life brought to complete stillness. Tiny lives; who knew—perhaps the birds died during the night and others rose in their place in the morning sun and flew away for the day's calls?

Ram Nath did not live only for these week-ends in the country. He passionately meant to do all he could to undo the evils that had fallen on India in its period of slavery, which he now saw clearly drawing to an end. He devoted a third of the profits from the soap factory to the building of model housing for the factory workers, and another portion of the profits he spent on a hospital, a school, and a nursery for the young children. The next step was to be a library, for which he would personally select the books, and then there would be playing-fields. Even after all these activities, he would still be making a handsome profit from his other interests, but he was convinced that, for the present at least, he would be justified in keeping the profits; later he could use the accumulation to start other enterprises.

At this juncture, some of the other soap-manufacturers asked him whether they could count on his support in a plea they were making for increased prices for their products.

Ram Nath was taken aback. He could see no reason why prices should be increased. He believed that the operating costs of many of the other factories were lower than his, and certainly the owners were not spending anything like the amount he was putting out on amenities for labour. He asked why they were asking for higher prices, and it turned out that the others thought that, as they had been on one price schedule for over a year, the time had come—on principle, they said—to ask for a small increase.

"What is the principle?" he asked.

"Well," said their spokesman. "You see, we should not lose an opportunity of making a little more money. After all, if there was no price control, maybe we could do better."

Ram Nath was amazed at this argument. The blood rushed to his face. He wanted to tell the rich owner of the soap factories that he ought to be kicked, but he controlled himself and simply asked the man to leave the house immediately; if he did not, he, Ram Nath, would be obliged to report his suggestion to the Government—even if it was only a foreign Government that was on its way out. The industrialist could hardly believe that his colleague was telling him to get out, but when he heard the threat that the Dewan added to his order, he decided it would be wisest to leave without any further argument.

Although he kept his word and did not report the matter to the Government, Ram Nath was not the sort of person who could hold his peace about an incident of this kind. The next time Jai visited him, he told him the story with great relish. Ram Nath added: "I am not going to have this country of ours played with by anti-social people. The British—well, everyone knows that they don't run this country for the good of the people, but they have not been too bad as administrators. Now we are turning them out, and I suppose we are doing so because we want a much better job done for the country by our own people. And then this son of deceit has the nerve to come and suggest a dirty deal to me!"

"Bravo, Dewanji! That will teach him a lesson. But the tragedy is that these people, who must know that the country is soon to be their own direct responsibility, should behave in this shameful way," observed Jai.

It was Friday. The Dewan was about to leave for Adampur, but, wanting to talk to Jai, he invited him to come with him in the car. Twice previously Jai had been taken to Adampur, and the Dewan had told him that the place was inviolate: never would he let any of his relatives know that he owned it. Even Dina Nath, his son, imagined that his father went to one of the neighbouring villages where they had land, or visited one of his cronies. The property deeds relating to Adampur had not been shown to anyone in the family.

During the journey the Dewan was in high spirits. He praised the estate and said that it had added ten years to his life. "Jai Singh, it is the apple of my eye. I never knew it would be; but it is even more: I feel its warmth in the very centre of my life. Remember that love is a wonderful thing. But it never comes in the way one might expect it to."

When they reached Adampur, Ram Nath sat still in the car for a minute or two. He was wondering whether he could now take Jai Singh into the house. Then he raised himself jerkily on his cane and, shaking his head, said aloud:

"Not just yet. Not just yet. I will see you tomorrow, Jai Singh. Namaskar!"

Two servants ran out to help the Dewan into the house. Then the car swung round. Jai felt that he knew what the

Dewan had meant by the words he had uttered on leaving the car: whenever the inroads of the unfamiliar threatened to become too deep, he would quietly go away to Adampur and return revived and alert. Jai was aware, too, that here, in this hidden spot, Ram Nath kept his mistress. But he knew that, important as was the tenderness he got from her, Adampur did much more for the Dewan. It was a kind of immersion in the unbroken past of India, into those traditions which the Dewan chose to keep alive for himself and which, when the tempo of political and other events in the country was eventually modulated, would give to those who cared for such things a beauty, depth, and perspective that participation in even the greatest events could furnish but feebly and in transience. Jai did not delve further into all this. He told himself that it was a part of life which Ram Nath wished to keep to himself, and he respected this reserve, for he had come to feel deeply affectionate toward the old man. But, in truth, there was a more direct reason for Jai's reluctance to explore fully his realization of what Adampur meant to Ram Nath. He had come to feel the emptiness of his own inner life so acutely that he shrank from the pain of this feeling. He felt defenceless against it and told himself that there seemed to be no escape for him from the existence he had chosen.

CHAPTER TWENTY-EIGHT

By 1942 events had made inevitable the final hard phase of the movement for the freedom of India. All over the great continent, the cry of the people went up against the foreign ruler. "Quit India!" It was heard on the steps of the Imperial Palace of the rulers at Delhi, by the gateway of India at Bombay, in the remotest village meeting-places, on the telephone wires, and in the songs of travelling minstrels. Throughout the country, never was the reverberation of the words silenced. "Quit India! Quit India!"

The British reacted as might have been expected of a disciplined government. They resorted once more to all the repertoire of governmental action: the leaders were hastily put in prison, the over-enthusiastic young people who carried on were shot down or apprehended, property was confiscated, and the country was reduced to a rough and harsh similitude of order.

When the older leaders had been arrested, the people of Delhi put Jai Singh in charge of the Movement in the city. The Commissioner gave orders that he was to be arrested the moment he led a procession in the city. Police cordons were strengthened on the routes that the processions normally took. It was expected that, under the leadership of this young man, all the younger generation in Delhi, who were now getting to know of Jai as a fearless person, would come out and demonstrate against the rulers. For the British, their position and prestige in Delhi—the centre of their Empire—was of crucial importance.

But Jai had no intention of leading a procession at this stage. He had long felt that the people in the villages should be brought more closely into the Movement, and now he could do something toward accomplishing this end. He organized twenty groups of city people, who went each day to the villages to talk to the people. The groups were small, and as the larger villages in the immediate vicinity of Delhi were at first excluded from their plan of work, the authorities did not immediately realize what was happening. While they continued to expect the procession, more and more villages were being visited. The farmers were eager to hear news of Gandhiji and Nehru and of the days when swarajya (the rule of the truth—Gandhiji's phrase) would be achieved.

Finally came the day fixed for the procession. The people from the surrounding villages and from the city knew that the hour of freedom had struck. The whole sky was filled with sound, and the clear air seemed to stand ready in a steely blue, while the buildings wore an ominous look as if expecting a great storm to break. The police by now had taken up their positions, though they had not yet been given clear orders as to what they were to do. The crowd surged past them, high-spirited but orderly and clearly not intent on damage or harm of any kind.

The procession was now approaching the grounds on which was held the annual celebration of the Ram Lila—the story of the triumph of good over evil, told in the epic Ramayana. Jai felt that, once they reached the grounds, all would be well: even the police were used to the crowds that gathered there each October, and surely they would not object to a meeting there today. Like a great unwieldy monster, the procession moved painfully slowly, and each inch of the way Jai felt the increasing weight of responsibility pressing upon him. But the police officer in charge was unaware of the precarious calculations that were filling Jai's thoughts. He decided that the procession had gone on long enough, and in a bored voice he shouted to his men the order to shoot. A great hole was torn in the middle of the procession. Jai and those with him stopped, and the women hurried to the fallen men and women. Some appeared to have been killed, for they lay still, but many groaned and the women quickly rushed to attend to them.

Seeing the crowd melt away after the dead and wounded had been removed, the police sprang into action again. They realized that soon everyone would have gone and they would have nothing left to show for what had happened: there had to be the guilty, and these could not be the police themselves. They came up to the few who were left and began to arrest them. Jai pleaded with them not to take those who were actually removing the casualties, and to this extent the police officer relented. But the remaining two hundred or so, including Jai Singh, were taken into custody and driven away in the closed grey police vans that had drawn up on the side.

Jai and his companions were driven to the Red Fort. Through the steel grille of the van, he could see the place bristling with British troops. Strange, he thought, that so much effort should be concentrated on these prisoners who were non-violent and who were certainly not going to attempt to break out.

During this period there was also trouble on the estates of the Dewan. The peasants had joined whole-heartedly in the Movement and had disarmed the police at the neighbouring police station. They took the rifles and made a bonfire, and the ammunition they threw into the river. They decided to use the building for a school, but the very next day a large posse of police was sent to take charge of the situation. They levied a fine on the whole village and proceeded to arrest all those who looked as though they might be ringleaders. This meant that the fields were neglected, and, on top of that, the men came to the Dewan and begged him to pay the fine. They claimed that, after all, they had only been acting in the interest of the country and should not have to pay a penalty.

At first the Dewan was in a fury at the men. Who had told them that they were to disarm the police? Did they think that was being non-violent? They were fools if they thought that they had done the right thing and that there was any chance of his paying the fine. Muttering to himself, Ram Nath turned on his heel and left the men.

But when he got to his room and sat in his favourite chair, he felt sick. The tempo of things had grown too swift for him. What was happening in the world? These docile people of the village had never done anything without discussing the matter first with him, and now they had gone and attacked the manifestation of the power of the foreign ruler.

It did not make sense. And then they felt that they had done right. He admitted to himself that they had some reason on their side, but the total picture was confusing. He felt the hair on his forehead tentalizing him. He brushed it away and sighed. Would he be able to make the transition from his world to this new confusion which was apparently the world of tomorrow? He felt sicker than before. His tongue was heavy and dry. This was no longer a lack of words with which to answer his own question, but a refusal from deep down in himself.

He lay very still, reclining in his chair. Overlapping images carried him into a perplexing reverie. There was himself, and there was the whole of India—and they were both trying to pass through a gay gateway such as is erected at festivals and marriages. He passed through, and that seemed very easy. But then the other half of the image was left, as though it had lost its capacity to float with him. He went back to the other side of the gate and, taking the image of India, he went with it to the gate—but no, there was not enough room. So he pushed the image of India and it floated gracefully through the gate into very beautiful blue space. He smiled and tried to step across into the loveliness beyond the gate, but he could not move. He argued with his feet. He looked at his shoes—they were well polished, and his English woollen socks were neat and in correct taste. So, he told himself, there was nothing wrong and of course he could pass the gate. But he remained immobilized. Feeling very tired, he gave up the struggle.

About an hour later he opened his eyes. He felt very weak. He rang for one of his men and then sent for his cashier.

"Are the men from the estate still outside?" he asked.

"Yes, Maharaj. They are waiting."

Ram Nath got up with his old quickness. "Good! Come with me," he said.

They went out on to the veranda. The men were sitting very quietly, as though ashamed to say anything for themselves. They remained sitting when the Dewan came out. He called to the headman and asked him what was the amount of the fine. The man stood up and told him.

Ram Nath turned to the cashier. "Give him the money, and see that the fine is paid."

All the men got up and said that their children would bless their Dewan. They held their hands together in greeting to him. He stood silently for a few moments, then raised his hands to them and silently turned away and went to his room.

Ram Nath did not feel at all well, and that evening he took to his bed. Next morning came the news of Gandhiji's release from prison. The country interpreted this news as the capitulation of the British Government to their leader.

CHAPTER TWENTY-NINE

IN THE late spring of 1944 Jai Singh was released from the district jail at Jullundhur. Acquaintances in the town gave him his fare to Delhi and a little extra for expenses. He set out at once, and from the railway station at Delhi he drove in a tonga directly to Dewan House. As the tonga slowly jogged through the streets, his eye picked out each stone and brick in the walls and even the tired dust on each leaf of the magnificent old peepul trees. Everything looked very old and run-down, as if carrying the full weight of a dying era. The tonga-driver, a man who had travelled these streets for the past twenty years, kept telling him how, all over the city, people were saying that the days of poverty would soon end and everyone would have four pieces of bread to eat each day—that was all they worried about. He said that there was a new smell in the air. Of course, some people were nervous, fearing that when the British left, things would be worse, not better. "But," added this philosopher, "there are always people who are upset by the smell of spring! They have weak lungs, and while most people are being filled with new life, they—poor things—complain of suffocation."

Something was about to happen. Everyone knew it, even those who doubted that it would be for the best. Jai looked again at the old bricks and the ancient trees. In their tiredness they appeared to him as symbols of the thirsty, hungry, long struggle for India's freedom which was now ending.

On arriving at Dewan House, Jai learned that Ram Nath was seriously ill. He had been more or less bedridden for almost six months. Sometimes he would insist on being driven by his chauffeur, Gangu, to Adampur, and on his return from these excursions he would appear to be alert and energetic again. He would give orders about the garden or the food and he would attend to his business affairs, seeming to recall exactly where he had left off perhaps ten days before. But he would tire quickly and, leaving things unfinished, he would take to his bed again for days on end.

Gangu took Jai to the Dewan's room. They looked in gingerly, not knowing whether he was asleep. But he was wide awake and immediately called to Gangu, who entered, bringing Jai with him.

Ram Nath looked up and, propping himself up, called in his quick, staccato manner: "Come in! Come in, Jai Singh! But where is Geeta? Oh, no, of course, she is married to her millionaire in Calcutta. . . ."

He sighed and stroked his little white beard. "I haven't been very well, Jai Singh. Nothing serious. I am getting up right away. I really feel all right, but when I go about and attend to things, they don't seem any longer to make sense. Even the house looks different—as if it were gaping at me.

The garden never looks its best—the soil has run down, I suppose. I don't know."

He lay back and rested for a while. Then he talked again.

"Till only the other day I thought all the answers were in modern astrophysics. And then, if you please, most of them—Eddington, Jeans, and the rest—suddenly started to say they knew very little and were not sure of more than a small percentage of what they had been saying. Fantastic! It was like the soil suddenly dying on me. Now where am I to turn? Tell me—perhaps you can. You have had so much to do with the making of the new India. You must know what you are making!" He stopped.

Jai wondered whether he should say something now. The old man was obviously deserted by all that had been his world—even Geeta. What could he, Jai, say that would give him hope and some peace? The silence continued. He would have to say something.

"Dewan, when I came in I thought the flowers and the lawns looked lovely—almost lovelier than ever," he tried lamely.

Ram Nath broke the silence that followed. "I don't think it is the flowers I am worried about. It is really what all this amounts to. I had hope in the flowers. I scolded the gardeners because I had that hope. But now I just couldn't do even that. Maybe it's old age, or maybe it's the thing that happens to us and brings on old age. You see, if I felt I was leaving something and going to something else—like I feel when I go to Adampur—then it would be all right. But I don't know where I am going. I might have got to know more about these things, but I didn't really give myself a chance. I thought I knew everything. No, not that. But I assumed that everything was in the books in my library. Well, that is where I went wrong." He stopped again.

Jai waited. He could say nothing at this point. He hoped that Ram Nath would fall asleep, but after a few moments the old man started to talk again.

"Perhaps it is in the books in the library. But books can't belong to one any more than the people who wrote them. Each of us must experience life for himself. All these books give us a wrong idea. We think we can read up our lives, while we really have to live them—and read along the way. I never had much use for people who did not read. But I never enquired what else they did. Maybe many of them were living much more than I, with all my reading and talking."

He stopped, and a thin wisp of a smile moved his lips. An idea had come to him. "Yes, one must live. I will go now to Adampur!" He insisted on getting up. He rang for his chauffeur, and Jai knew that he should leave. He went up to the Dewan to make his salutations. Ram Nath held Jai's hand and, taking him toward his bureau, he said tensely: "Wait. There is something you are to take."

Ram Nath opened the bureau and took out a sealed envelope. He handed it to Jai, saying: "Yes. You can go now, Jai Singh. Open this when I—when I can't tell you not to."

Jai understood. He raised his hands in a namaskar. Ram Nath nodded and smiled faintly.

Then Ram Nath made his last journey into life. It was a good journey. His beautiful mistress looked after him with great tenderness. To her, and in her tradition, old age was a guest just as much as youth. Both the guests she entertained and respected. That evening Ram Nath was happier than

ever before. Things became clearer to him. He knew that
there was a certain sense in dying. He realized that the
flowers had quite rightly stopped looking at him because
they knew his time was up. If he were to stay on, he would
hold up the others—his own son, who had never been able to
grow up because of his domination; his second daughter,
whom he had held captive this last year instead of letting her
live her own life. He no longer worried as to what it would
be like in the new India. That was for those who would
come after him. He was full of his own days, and, with
them, he really ought now to retire. The only thing in life
which touched him deeply was the tenderness of this beautiful young woman Zohra, who understood that his days
were over. She remained truly close to him because she did
understand and was courageous, while the others were too
frightened to tell him that he had lived his life. There was
no point in going back to them.

As the week-end closed, Ram Nath fell into a coma. His
chauffeur took him home. For two days he lingered quietly and peacefully. Then he died, and Dewan House went
into mourning.

CHAPTER THIRTY

FOR SEVERAL DAYS after the death of Dewan Ram Nath, various organizations in Delhi convened meetings and adopted respectfully worded resolutions lamenting the loss of an outstanding, much-loved, and exemplary citizen and gentleman. The Bar Association, the Municipality, the Brahmin Association, the University Senate, the Sanatana Dharma Sabha, the Chamber of Commerce, the Grain Merchants Association, the Fruit Merchants Association, and the Landlords Association were but a few of those that indited their homage to the memory of the Dewan in fulsome phrases. Though Ram Nath had taken no part in the national struggle, some of the tributes to him even lauded his work for the Freedom Movement and expressed regret that he had been removed from the stage just as India was entering upon its freedom.

In one capacity or another, even Jai, whose life had not been lived within the main conventional currents, found

himself at meetings to honour the worthy man. He had become closely acquainted with the Dewan, which could not
be said of most of those who now, mainly because they
sought prominence for themselves, framed resolutions or
made speeches. Jai felt that in all this the poor Dewan was
being reduced to a few trite words, and he was amazed at
the capacity of people to lose the essence of that which they
professed to admire and love.

However, it was the busy season and Jai soon found all
his time taken up by the law courts and unending meetings
that were being held to consider and plan the future of
the country. The days carried Jai along in their full sweep,
and it was not till about two weeks after Ram Nath's death
that it occurred to him to open the sealed envelope which
the Dewan had given him at their last meeting. It contained
a signed statement from Ram Nath to the effect that the
Adampur estate had been bequeathed to him, free of all
encumbrances; and that, furthermore, the Registrar of Properties in Delhi had been informed accordingly. Jai read the
document again. There was no ambiguity. The next morning he called at the office of the Registrar of Properties and
found that a deed had been registered recording the transfer
of the property to him.

Still without any feeling of connection with Ram Nath's
bequest, but with his curiosity roused, Jai hired a car and
drove to Adampur. The car soon was jolting along the private driveway shaded with ancient mango, loquat, and lime
trees. Jai felt that he was being immersed in a strange depth,
and for the first time he really looked at the estate. His eyes
picked out things, such as the brick-work of the culverts and
the large pottery vases, which were the handiwork of earlier
generations, and he began to realize that the scene before

him was the result of careful tending over perhaps several centuries. Even the bark of the trees, hard and smooth as horn, seemed to belong to another age. It was only now that Jai noticed the handsomely carved, broad, red sandstone lintels of the main doorway and its setting of old, smooth brick-work.

Hearing the car approach the brick terrace, the caretaker came to the door. First the old man, with his henna-dyed beard, peered doubtfully at Jai, who was walking toward the house. Then he recognized the new master: for he had been informed by the Dewan that the property was being left to Jai.

They exchanged greetings and the old man talked fondly about the Dewan. The words strung from his lips, and though they had a formal quality, there was also in them a deep sincerity, as there might be in the repetition of a mantra or the paternoster. Jai said that he would like to look around alone. The caretaker bent low and withdrew.

Jai walked through the first courtyard and along the main veranda with its beautiful arches of handsomely cut red sandstone. He went through several rooms with lofty ceilings and beautifully designed clerestories till he came to the stairway in the central hall. It was narrow and steep, with no banisters, in the architectural style of the eighteenth century.

On the next floor, the rooms were beautifully ventilated and the green light from the leafy trees streamed in. Jai climbed another flight of stairs to the roof terrace. The paving was of smooth tiles—deep red with white piping. A low trellised wall of red sandstone enclosed three sides of the terrace, while on the western side, overlooking the formal garden behind the house, the trellis was of exquisite white marble, almost translucent. In the southwest corner was a walled pavilion—a room that could hold a large mattress and a table with a little space to spare. It was beautifully designed, with graceful, wing-like, sloping eaves sweeping upward to a low domed roof.

Jai entered the pavilion. The walls were of white lime cement, so highly polished that they gleamed like a liquid surface. And—delightful surprise—on the wall before him a mural of gaily painted horsemen and, as he turned, on the opposite wall a dancer with her musicians. The old paintings glowed in ochre, burnt sienna, lapis-lazuli, gold, verte, and red. On the perfect surface, they had retained the liveliness that the artist had put into them perhaps two centuries ago. As Jai stood there, unable to take his eyes off them, they seemed to tear away the curtains of time which had bound him. When he went out on to the open terrace again, he felt a sense of emergence, as though a restraining hand had been withdrawn from his shoulder, snatching away the wraps in which he had lived.

Jai looked over the marble trellis at the formal garden with its rose beds and the central row of miniature fountains from which the water tinkled musically into a long, shallow pool. Beyond, there was the tangled depth of the closely planted orchard, shutting off the heart of the estate from its outlying farmlands.

Jai realized that he had not merely entered the heart of a past age. It was as if he was in the midst of an enduring movement; that which continued from the past and the present, and that which would continue from the future were here gathered and gathering together. He did not feel alienated from the political movement in which he had been so deeply absorbed, but now he knew also that the richness under the surface was not to be neglected in the movement forward. He experienced this knowledge directly as he stood looking over the marble trellis and breathing freshness from the continuing past. He smiled at himself for having been so deeply engrossed in the immediate act of movement that he had not stopped to comprehend the fullness of that which was moving forward. He stood still, and, in the stillness, he felt himself growing in strength and in his capacity for life. Again he filled his being with the age-distilled richness of Adampur.

Jai descended the steep steps of the stairway and, hearing the sound of the bells of tonga horses, went through the courtyard to the main gate. Workmen, probably gardeners from the estate, were piling luggage into two tongas that stood on the stone pavement. Then, from the side rooms that he had not yet visited, emerged two musicians, carrying their instruments, and a dancer, who followed them slowly, wistfully. The woman turned and saluted him before she entered the tonga. The carriages drove away, and Jai Singh and Adampur were left to each other.

A NOTE ON THE TYPE

This book was set on the Linotype in GRANJON, a type named in compliment to Robert Granjon, but neither a copy of a classic face nor an entirely original creation. George W. Jones based his designs for this type upon the type used by Claude Garamond (1510–61) in his beautiful French books, and Granjon more closely resembles Garamond's own than do any of the various modern types that bear his name.

Robert Granjon began his career as type-cutter in 1523. The boldest and most original designer of his time, he was one of the first to practise the trade of type-founder apart from that of printer. Between 1557 and 1562 Granjon printed about twenty books in types designed by himself, following, after the fashion of the day, the cursive handwriting of the time. These types, usually known as "caractères de civilité," he himself called "lettres françaises," as especially appropriate to his own country.

Composed, printed, and bound by H. Wolff, New York. Paper made by S. D. Warren Company, Boston, Massachusetts. Drawings by John Teppich. Designed by Harry Ford.